# TARGET LIZZY
## FALLING FOR HIS BADASS

A FEW GOOD MEN
BOOK ONE

JESSIKA KLIDE WRITING AS
STINGRAY23

# AUTHOR'S COPYRIGHT

This is a work of fiction. Names, characters, organizations, places, events, and incidents are either products of the author's imagination or are used fictitiously. Any resemblance to actual events, locales, or persons living or dead are entirely coincidental.

Copyright © 2023 Stingray23 ALL RIGHTS RESERVED

No part of this book may be reproduced, or stored in a retrieval system, or transmitted in any form or by any means electronic, mechanical, photocopying, recording, or otherwise, without express written permission of the publisher.

This book is licensed for your personal enjoyment only. This book may not be re-sold or given away to other people.

Editing by: Maria Clark

Formatting by: Jessika Klide, LLC

Published in the United States of America

HUMAN TRAFFICKING HAPPENS EVERYWHERE. TO MEN, WOMEN, AND CHILDREN OF ALL AGES, RACES, NATIONALITIES, AND GENDERS.

*DONATE TO MAKE A DIFFERENCE: OURRESCUE.ORG*

IF YOU OR SOMEONE YOU KNOW IS A VICTIM OF HUMAN TRAFFICKING, REACH OUT FOR HELP OR REPORT A TIP NOW.

NATIONAL HUMAN TRAFFICKING HOTLINE
**1-888-373-7888**

TEXT **"BEFREE"** OR **"HELP"** TO 233733

EMAIL: HELP@HUMANTRAFFICKINGHOTLINE.ORG

NATIONAL CENTER FOR MISSING OR EXPLOITED CHILDREN
**1-800-THE-LOST**

# CONTENTS

| | |
|---|---|
| The Navy Seal Creed | 7 |
| Chapter 1 | 13 |
| Chapter 2 | 19 |
| Chapter 3 | 27 |
| Chapter 4 | 39 |
| Chapter 5 | 45 |
| Chapter 6 | 51 |
| Chapter 7 | 57 |
| Chapter 8 | 67 |
| Chapter 9 | 75 |
| Chapter 10 | 83 |
| Chapter 11 | 89 |
| Chapter 12 | 97 |
| Chapter 13 | 107 |
| Chapter 14 | 115 |
| Chapter 15 | 121 |
| Chapter 16 | 129 |
| Chapter 17 | 135 |
| Chapter 18 | 143 |
| Epilogue | 151 |

| | |
|---|---|
| Jessika writing as Stingray23 | 171 |
| Jessika writing as Cindee Bartholomew | 173 |
| Read Jessika's newest, sexiest, and most talked about bestsellers... | 175 |
| Stingray23 | 179 |
| Stingray23.com | 181 |

# THE NAVY SEAL CREED

IN TIMES OF WAR OR UNCERTAINTY THERE IS A SPECIAL BREED OF WARRIOR READY TO ANSWER OUR NATION'S CALL. A COMMON MAN WITH UNCOMMON DESIRE TO SUCCEED.

FORGED BY ADVERSITY, HE STANDS ALONGSIDE AMERICA'S FINEST SPECIAL OPERATIONS FORCES TO SERVE HIS COUNTRY, THE AMERICAN PEOPLE, AND PROTECT THEIR WAY OF LIFE.

I AM THAT MAN.

MY TRIDENT IS A SYMBOL OF HONOR AND HERITAGE. BESTOWED UPON ME BY THE HEROES THAT HAVE GONE BEFORE, IT EMBODIES THE TRUST OF THOSE I HAVE SWORN TO PROTECT. BY WEARING THE TRIDENT, I ACCEPT THE RESPONSIBILITY OF MY CHOSEN PROFESSION AND WAY OF LIFE. IT IS A PRIVILEGE THAT I MUST EARN EVERY DAY.

My loyalty to Country and Team is beyond reproach. I humbly serve as a guardian to my fellow Americans always ready to defend those who are unable to defend themselves. I do not advertise the nature of my work, nor seek recognition for my actions. I voluntarily accept the inherent hazards of my profession, placing the welfare and security of others before my own.

I serve with honor on and off the battlefield. The ability to control my emotions and my actions, regardless of circumstance, sets me apart from other men.

Uncompromising integrity is my standard. My character and honor are steadfast. My word is my bond.

We expect to lead and be led. In the absence of orders, I will take charge, lead my teammates, and accomplish the mission. I lead by example in all situations.

I will never quit. I persevere and

thrive on adversity. My Nation expects me to be physically harder and mentally stronger than my enemies. If knocked down, I will get back up, every time. I will draw on every remaining ounce of strength to protect my teammates and to accomplish our mission. I am never out of the fight.

We demand discipline. We expect innovation. The lives of my teammates and the success of our mission depend on me — my technical skill, tactical proficiency, and attention to detail. My training is never complete.

We train for war and fight to win. I stand ready to bring the full spectrum of combat power to bear in order to achieve my mission and the goals established by my country. The execution of my duties will be swift and violent when required yet guided by the very principles that I serve to defend.

Brave men have fought and died building the proud tradition and feared reputation that I am bound to uphold.

In the worst of conditions, the legacy of my teammates steadies my resolve and silently guides my every deed.

I will not fail.

# TARGET LIZZY

# CHAPTER ONE

*Lizzy*

---

"But why?" I ask my best friend, Tara. "Why do I have to go with you?"

"Two reasons. One, you need to get out of the house. You've been sulking around long enough. Jack was an ass and didn't deserve a single minute more of your time." She sits next to me and puts her arm around me. "I hate seeing you like this." She hugs me tight, and I lay my head on her shoulder. "Lizzy, you deserve better."

"My heart is tired of hurting," I confess.

"You need a change of scenery *and* selection."

Tara and I have been best friends since college, and this isn't the first time she's seen me down in the dumps over a dude. Some of the men I've dated, she's liked, and some, she hasn't. Jack was one she never liked, and she was right. He was a decent dude but a total dud.

I ask my best friend. "What's the second reason for going with you?"

"I don't want to go alone," she smirks. "Please?"

"Ah," I laugh, "the truth comes out."

Her eyes twinkle, "Please come, Lizzy. It'll be fun, I promise."

"I don't know." I try not to capitulate too easily. "What will I do while you are busy being John's latest conquest?"

"Last. I'm going to be busy being John's *last* conquest." She corrects me while her mischievous grin smiles at me.

I nod and reword my question. "What will I do while you are busy being John's *last* conquest?"

"Why don't you go to The Lost Boys dinner show?"

"Tara," I hug her, knowing she has given getting me out of my apartment a lot of thought, "that's an excellent idea!" I pick my phone up off the coffee table. "If I can get a ticket, I'll come with you."

She leans across the space and hugs me tight. "You can. They aren't sold out Friday night."

I laugh with her. "You're the best!"

"I know."

\* \* \*

Three days later, Tara pulls up outside my apartment and my phone dings.

*I'm here. Do you need help?*

*No. Be right down.*

I grab my backpack, look around my apartment, then lock the door.

When I slide into the front seat next to her, she flashes her cute smile, and her eyes twinkle as she greets me. "There's my beautiful bestie. Glad to see your happy face is back."

I grin, "No more Jack-asses for me! Let's go!"

"Atta a girl!"

She backs out of the parking spot, puts the car in drive, and we leave our small town for the city and John's house.

Tara and John met six months ago at the

Medical Center, where she is a nurse. He is a pharmaceutical representative and was there pushing a new drug to a staff doctor. Tara barged in on their meeting to announce that the doctor's wife had been in a car accident and was admitted to the emergency room. The doctor left Tara to handle the transaction, she and John went out that night, and they've been dating since.

During the miles and miles of interstate highway, Tara and I talk about my dating woes. "So, what's your advice for me this weekend? I'm obviously doing something wrong to keep getting Love-Bombed." I ask her.

"Don't go out looking for love." She cuts her eyes at me. "Just go out dancing to unwind. Have fun."

I nod. "I will. My heart isn't ready for anyone new. It's tired of being strung along."

"Lizzy, you have to stop worrying about finding the right guy. He's just going to show up."

I cut my eyes at her. "How am I supposed to know who he is? A lot of guys show up."

"Your heart will know." She states. I almost laugh at her, but I know she is serious, and I would never hurt her feelings. "Even if a dude is digging you, and he's a good catch if your heart doesn't react," she cuts her eyes at me again, "Not respond. But react as soon as you see him. Then he's not the one."

I mull over her answer. I've been with men that stirred my heart, but was it a response or a reaction?

"Is that what happened with John?" I study her.

As good friends as we are, she never told me how she felt the first time they met, only the story of how they met. "Did your heart react?"

She laughs, "As soon as John smiled at me, my heart went nuts. I knew right then that if he asked me out, I would say yes. By the end of the transaction, I knew that if he didn't ask me, I would ask him."

"Wow!" I'm surprised by her answer.

Tara is a very reserved, shy person, and the fact that she intended to be bold and ask him out herself shocks me. "It was that fast?"

She nods. "It was. The more I get to know him, the *better* he gets too." She grins so big I can't help but believe her.

"Love looks good on you," I state.

# CHAPTER
# TWO

The GPS tells us to take the next off-ramp, and our conversation ends. As Tara skillfully maneuvers the directions being issued, I think about what she has described. I've never believed in love at first sight, but it seems real if Tara and John are proof.

The closer we get, the more excited she becomes, and the brighter her star shines. But as soon as we turn onto John's street, we see a candy apple red Corvette parked in front of his house, and her status shifts from star to stalker in a split second. She blurts out as if I have a clue. "Whose car is that?"

"How should I know?" I blurt out, too, "but it's a dope ride!"

She cuts scared eyes at me.

"Maybe it's John's." I offer, but we both know it's not. He's not a 'vet' kind of guy. He's conservative, and guys who drive vets like to go fast. Otherwise, what's the point?

"It's not John's." She states, for the record. She pulls into the driveway and tells me, "Don't shut your door when you get out, Lizzy. Just push it till it latches."

"Seriously?" I look at her. She is on full bitch alert. "Do you think he's going to cheat on you when he knows you are coming for a visit? Take my word for it, Tara. They cheat when they don't know you're coming."

She cuts her eyes at me, and her look says it all. She didn't tell John she was coming.

"What the fuck, Tara? He doesn't know?"

"He knows I'm coming, just not a day early. I was supposed to drive up tomorrow morning. I thought I would surprise him." She looks wild-eyed, and I realize this could go sideways quickly. Tara is a redhead with a fiery temper and cheating scars.

"Oh, dear lord!" I reach over and grab the steering wheel. "No fucking way are we walking in unannounced!"

Beep. Beep. I smack the horn.

She slaps my hand away, looking both scared and angry. "Lizzy! Stop!"

"No, John loves you." I smack the horn twice more. "He's done nothing to deserve jealousy. That's a leftover scar from Jimmy."

We stare defiantly at each other for a moment, then she blinks, "Fine," opens her door, and gets out.

"Fine," I open my door as well, but before I can stand, the front door opens, and John's handsome mug appears on the front porch.

His smile says it all. Tara *is* going to be his last conquest. "BAE!" He shouts and opens his arms. "Wow! What a wonderful surprise!"

All doubt and jealousy disappear from Tara, and she runs to him, shining as brightly as before. When she arrives, she jumps into his arms, and he swings her around while she showers him with kisses.

I slowly close the car door and lean against it, watching them. I sigh. I want that. I want an all-consuming love. The kind of love that makes you crazy.

When their lips finally unlock, they both

turn to beam at me. I wave, laughing, happy they are together. "Hi, John."

"Hi, Lizzy!" John smiles as he sets her down, taking her hand and walking to the car. "I'm so glad you're here. This is perfect!" He grins at me. "You can meet my little brother."

*Little brother?* My eyes dart to glare at Tara. *I am NOT babysitting.*

Tara catches my look, then playfully pushes him away. "Brother? I didn't know you had a little brother."

"Yeah, he popped in unannounced on his way to a new assignment last night." He pulls her tight against him again. Tara's eyes glaze over as she slips her arms around his waist. He cuts his eyes at me and winks. "He's in the military."

I smile sweetly at John as he releases Tara and walks to the back of the car to get our bags. "I'm not staying," I tell him firmly. "I'm just dropping her off. I have a ticket to catch 'The Lost Boys Dinner Show' tonight. I've been dying to see it, and Jack wouldn't take me. Thanks for the offer, though, but I'll pass."

He throws her bag over his shoulder and says, as he closes the door. "You should reconsider. He's a really great guy."

I smirk, "I'm sure he is, but I've made plans." I hold my hand out to Tara. "Keys, please?"

Tara shoves the car keys down her jeans pocket and frowns at me. "Lizzy, don't be rude. At least, come inside to meet him." She slips her hand back into John's and walks with him to the house.

I bite my tongue and watch them whispering to each other, and I wonder if this was a conspiracy to hook his brother and me up. When she dangles her car keys, I sigh as I follow them. I can't go anywhere without those. I raise my voice so they can hear me. "I can't stay long. I don't want to be late for the show."

Tara looks back, grinning, and mouths to me. "John's brother is a military man, Lizzy! How exciting!"

I mouth back, "This better not be a setup."

She grins, and I can't tell if it is or not.

When we walk into the house, I'm impressed with John's decor. It's not a bachelor pad. It's a home. He sets her bag down and points the way to the first-floor bathroom. "If you need to go potty, it's down the hall there."

I make a beeline for it.

When I return, John and Tara are preparing

to make margaritas in the kitchen. He tells me, "Brody's gone for a run."

I look at my phone to check the time. "I've only got a little time; then I must bug out."

He nods, takes his phone out, and starts to text someone, who I assume is Brody, as he asks me, "Margarita?"

I laugh, "No, thanks. I'm driving, remember?"

He chuckles and says, "My little brother is a great guy!"

I grin at that, pulling up a stool. "I'm sure he is. If I don't meet him before I leave, I'll make sure to come back in time on Sunday to meet him before we go home."

Tara asks as she mixes the Margaritas, "So tell us about your little brother? What's he do in the military?"

"I have no idea what he does. And, no idea where he does it. And, no idea when he will have to do it. And, no idea when he's done doing it and will come home."

"Oh," Tara mouths as her eyebrows raise. "He's a badass then."

He nods and chuckles. "Yeah, he's the badass of the family."

I laugh, "That's his corvette, then."

He chuckles harder. "Hell yeah, he's proud of that beauty too. He took me for a spin yesterday and nearly made me scream."

We all laugh at that.

"How long has Brody been in the service?" I ask.

"Too long, if you ask me, but about six years."

"Wow, hard-core," Tara says, then turns the blender on and mixes the batch of Margaritas. She pours the first one, and John slides it across the bar to me, grinning sheepishly. I smile, amused, but slide it back, shaking my head.

Tara play slaps him. "Lizzy will never forgive me if you keep trying to hook her up."

John laughs. "Brody will never forgive me if I don't."

My alarm on my phone goes off. "Well, it's time to go." I jump off the stool.

I look to Tara for support. Her eyes narrow when she reads my silent plea, so she says, "I'll walk you out."

"John, I'll come back Sunday around ten o'clock to get Tara, and I can meet Brody then."

He nods, clearly disappointed, but doesn't argue. Instead, he opens a bag of chips to munch on them.

Tara and I walk into the foyer as she attempts to persuade me, "I wish you ...."

When we hear tapping on the patio door, her voice drops off as John walks across the tile floor. I quickly grab Tara's arm and drag her out the front door.

On the way to the car, she says, "Lizzy, stay. If John says he's a great guy, he's a great guy."

"He may very well be, but if he isn't," I roll my eyes at her, "I'll be stuck all weekend pretending he's a great guy." I give her my best pleading expression and pout.

Her expression matches mine, but she nods, "I get it. I wish I could persuade you, but...."

"Thanks," I grab her in a you're-the-best hug, step back and hold my hand out. "Keys, please."

She laughs, "I'm tempted to deny you anyway."

I snatch them from her hand, then run around to the driver's side.

She shakes her phone at me. "Check in."

"I will," I tell her as I slide behind the wheel.

"Have fun!" She yells as I pull off.

I throw my hand up and escape.

# CHAPTER THREE

**Brody**

---

The steady beat of my feet hitting the pavement and the matching rhythm of my breath have always calmed me. I run because I have to, but that doesn't mean I don't enjoy it.

Five miles into my run, my phone vibrates. I pull it out of my pocket. It's John.

ETA?

30.

> *30 minutes? Bro, you need to return ASAP.*

> Sup?

> *Trust me!*

I slow to a jog, frowning.

> What is wrong?

> *Nothing is wrong. Something is right.*

> What?

I'm confused by his answer.

> Not what. Who! Turn around and come back now!

> Who?

> *Just hurry, Hotshot!*

I whip around and head back. If John thinks it is important enough to call me back to the house, that's good enough for me. I take off at a good clip.

Although John and I are blood brothers, we are very different. He's a nerd but one hell of a great salesman. I'm a jock and one hell of a badass. My mind drifts back to all the shit we shared growing up. He would get into trouble, and I would get him out. Good times.

Turning onto his street, I slow to a jog to cool down. I can see a black Honda parked in the driveway. As I walk by, I look in. There's a girl's backpack lying on the backseat. Ah! The who must be his new girl, Tara. He didn't mention she would be coming this weekend, but then again, John wouldn't. He knows I would bail on him and call Jeff to get a hotel room. Then he would lecture me about spending time with him while I was here and remind me that my job is dangerous. I love my brother but being single and hanging out with a couple isn't my thing. Three's a crowd.

I head to the rear of the house to take a dip in the pool. I don't want to be sweaty when introduced to his new girl. Rounding the corner, I hear John's voice through the breakfast nook window. It's open about an inch. Then I hear not one girl's voice but two, —laughing.

Oh, man, this sucks. Tara's brought someone along. I roll my eyes and sigh. John knows better than to set me up with a woman, but Tara doesn't. I walk over to the window to listen. Yep, they are talking about me. Damn. I've fended off aggressive female friends of friends before who only want to get laid by a Navy S.E.A.L. That's not what I'm about. As a behavioral specialist, I see right past all the games they play pretending they are into me when all they are into is a hard fuck from Badass so they can brag later to their bitches. Still, he is my brother and digs this Tara chick, and I haven't been laid in a while.

I bend down to peek through the window to scope out the friend. If she's not my type, petite, and very curvy, I'll call Jeff and bail to the hotel. If she is, I'll consider taking one for the team.

John and a tall, skinny chick with short red hair, who must be Tara based on how John is fawning over her, are standing at the bar mixing what looks like Margaritas. The other female is sitting across from them with her back to me. All I can see of her is her thick, long brown hair with soft curls that sway as she talks with her hands. Not bad so far.

A phone alarm goes off. The friend looks down at her lap to silence the notification. Then as she swings around on the barstool to face me, she kicks her tanned, shapely legs and jumps off the stool, landing gracefully in a pair of 6" high wedge sandals. She's wearing a barely buttoned shirt tied in a knot at her waist and a pair of short shorts with a waistline below her navel. The patch of skin exposed above shows off ample assets, and the patch below accentuates her toned abs. She bends over, flipping her thick mane to secure it into a bun.

While she works on her hair, I watch her heavy rack trying to escape her shirt. When her hair is secured, she stands up, and I smile. She's short, even in heels, and has generous curves in the right places.

Not bad at all. She's definitely doable.

I can see her face clearly with her soft, bouncy brown curls on top of her head. Her heart-shaped face has full brows that accentuate dark eyes. Her dainty nose sits above lips that are naturally pouty and downright kissable. She flashes a smile before turning to speak to Tara and John, and in that flash, I see her personality. She's bubbly, sweet, kind, and good to her core.

Staring at her very curvy, toned ass, I grin. Whew, Baby. That chick is something very right. I feel like a dog who's discovered a bitch in heat. Then she and Tara walk out, and I watch the graceful gait of her rolling ass.

I stride to the patio door to turn the handle, but it's locked. Damn. I cup my hands on the glass and peer into the room. John's eyes are glued on the twitching asses too, so I tap the glass lightly. He looks up, and when he sees me, he hurries over to the door and unlocks it.

"Brody, Good. You made it back in time. Tara and her roomie Lizzy arrived right after you left."

I glare at him. "That hot chick is Tara's roommate? How long have you known about her?"

He smirks, then steps outside with me, closing the door for privacy. "She was seeing someone."

"And now she's not?" I grin.

"Now, she's available." A smile spreads across his face. "I thought she was your type."

"Hell yeah, she's totally my type."

John opens the door. "Come on. Let me introduce you two."

"Hang on. I'm sweaty." I turn and run to the pool, pulling my shirt off on the way. At the edge, I shuck my shoes and dive in. When I surface, he calls from the doorway. "She's about to leave. Hurry up."

"Leave?" I swim to the edge and hoist myself out. "What the fuck? Where's she going?" But John isn't standing in the doorway any longer. He's back inside. Dripping wet, I run after him. He isn't in the kitchen, so I continue to the foyer. I can hear him in the bathroom. Wanting to watch Lizzy, I walk to the window, ease the curtain back, and stare at the two friends talking in front of the Honda.

John calls from the bathroom. "I'm getting you a towel."

"Why is Lizzy leaving?" I ask as John comes out and throws the towel at me.

"Drape that over your shoulders. Your massive chest makes me look wimpy." He shakes his head. "Dude, you just keep getting bigger and bigger."

I towel dry my hair first and ask again. "Why is Lizzy leaving?"

He answers while walking to the front door to wait for me. "Probably, the same reason you wouldn't have hung around when Tara showed up. Three's a crowd." John pulls the door open enough to see the girls. "I told her she could hang with you, but she had already bought a ticket to see 'The Lost Boys' at Jeff's place. Trust me. I tried to get her to change her mind. I told her what a great guy you are." He looks back at me. I have the towel draped over my shoulders. He shakes his head. "Fuck.... You're a damn beast. How much do you weigh now?"

"240." I step forward, ignoring him, and ease the window curtain back again. Lizzy snatches the keys from Tara and darts away. Something about the way she moves stirs something inside me. I watch as she playfully dangles the keys at Tara from a safe distance, then backs her way to the driver's door and opens it. I drop the curtain and look at my brother.

"What's wrong?" He asks, closing the door softly.

"Nothing's wrong," I smirk. "Someone is very right." I shove the towel back in his arms, then sprint up the steps.

He calls after me. "Where are you going?"

At the top, I stop and look at him. "With her."

Grabbing my rucksack, I quickly pack it for the weekend, then take it with me into the bathroom. I turn the water on as I load my toiletries, then strip, step in the shower, quickly soap my body, rinse, dry, dress, and in a matter of

# TARGET LIZZY

10 minutes, I'm heading back down the stairs. I can hear Tara and John in the kitchen. Leaving without saying goodbye, I trot to my Corvette and text John.

> What is Lizzy's last name?

> MAYER.

> BE BACK SUNDAY.

> HAVE FUN.

I toss my bag in the passenger seat, crank my car, then take off after her. Keeping my eyes focused, looking for the black Honda, I speed down the highway and instruct the vehicle to call Jeff.

Jeff's an old friend and former operator. I spent a lot of time with him before enlisting. It was his influence that steered me to become a SEAL.

When he answers, "Crockett, here," I tell him I need to grab a room for the weekend.

"No problem, man. You can stay as long as you like."

"Thanks, brother. I need you to do me a favor too. A couple of them, actually."

"Ask. You know I'll do whatever I can."

"I need you to put me in a room as close to Lizzy Mayer's as possible, and I need a ticket to the dinner show."

He chuckles. "Does Miss Mayer, or is it Mrs., have a ticket to the dinner show too?"

I laugh out loud. "It is Miss, and yes, she does."

"Standby." He tells me. I spot the Honda and match her pace, keeping several cars between us so she doesn't know she's being tailed. When Jeff comes back on the phone, he tells me. "All set. You're in the room next to hers and sitting at her table for the show. The show starts in an hour. How far out are you?"

"Fifteen, if I don't get stuck in traffic."

"We'll catch up on the unit later then. Your ticket and a VIP pass for the bar will be waiting for you at the door. Drinks are on me."

"You're too good to me," I tell him. "Thanks."

"Looking forward to your mission recap. I want all the sick details! Crockett, out here."

The call disconnects. I'm seven cars behind Lizzy when she exits the interstate. She flows through the green light at the bottom of the off-ramp, but I get caught when it changes to red. As

I watch her disappear out of sight, my gut involuntary reacts. My thumbs start to tap the steering wheel.

When it's my turn at the light, I follow her path, keeping a moderate pace.

**CHAPTER**
# FOUR

*Lizzy*

---

I grab my backpack and waltz into the hotel lobby when I arrive. The woman behind the counter takes my information and gives me my room key, #230, and my ticket to the dinner show then invites me to take advantage of the bar on the top floor called *Suds After BUD/S*. "We have a DJ tonight, and the place will be hopping. Just use your keycard to gain elevator access up to the bar."

Thanking her, I head to the elevator to wait. Suddenly, multiple doors down the corridor open, and voices flood the silence. A crowd of people laughing, talking louder than necessary, rounds the corner. Most of them pass by, but ten men in their thirties join me to wait for the elevator. When it arrives, I step forward first and enter. Completely ignoring them and avoiding eye contact, I stand at the panel.

While sharing the ride up, I learned they are lawyers at a conference and intend to skip the dinner show instead of going straight to the bar to begin drinking.

I'm the only one getting off when the elevator stops on my floor. As I excuse myself to gain access to exit, their conversation halts. I can feel their eyes on me, and as I walk away, I hear someone inside say, "I'm calling dibs." Then the others laugh.

I smile. Tonight should be fun.

My room is big and spacious, with a small sitting area. The bed is king-size. It has a small cocktail table and two armchairs.

"Sweet!" Tossing my backpack on it, I spin around and fall backward. It feels good to be free from Jack.

In the shower, I give myself a pep talk Tara would be proud to hear. "Ok, Miss Liza Jane, there will be a bar full of men. Good guys with good jobs. But you will only dance the night away and have fun."

Drying off, I continue my pep talk to my reflection as I apply foundation and eye shadow. "Nothing more. Unless, of course, there is a man that knocks you off your feet, steals your breath away, and your heart goes nuts over. Not the guy your mind calculates is a good match. So, dance only with the lawyers. No sex!"

Next, I apply mascara, stopping now and then to de-clump my lashes. "If you want an all-consuming love like Tara has, you're going to have to find the man that makes your heart go nuts."

I slip on matching panties to the red push-up bra that sets my tits on a shelf. Then pull the dress over my head and wiggle into it. It's a tad tight. "Honestly, the odds are against you. So... have a good time, but return to your room alone. You won't find him. He will have to find you."

I decide to run a flat iron through my thick hair so that it will fan out nicely when I twirl around on the dance floor.

I walk out to examine myself in the full-length mirror. The dress hugs my full figure like a glove but is definitely tighter than the last time I wore it. Twisting around to view the back, I frown. Panty lines are killing the rearview. Commando, then. I slip the red lace panties off and toss them on the couch. Then I recheck the view, smooth the fabric over my big butt, and smile, feeling beautiful.

I shove my keycard, credit card, and identification into my cleavage, pat them to be sure they don't move, then I step into my platform black pumps.

Checking my reflection one last time, I open the door and stroll down the hall toward the elevator. The heavy room door closes with a resounding echo down the corridor, and I confirm my shift in attitude. I am not hunting. I am the hunted, and my luck is about to change.

---

## Brody

---

Once I reach the hotel, I circle the block and enter the rear parking lot from the service entrance. I laugh at the sign that points the way to the dive bar. It reads, 'Leave Hell Behind, This Way to *Suds After BUD/S*.'

I hear the music from the dance floor as I leave the car. The place is already jamming. Grabbing my rucksack, I head inside.

"B.A!"

Looking up, I wave at Jeff. "Yo, Rocket!"

Jeff is leaning over the patio railing. "I'll be waiting for your update."

"Looking forward to it. It was a good mission."

Entering the lobby with the crowd from the lawyer's convention, I scan the area for Lizzy and see her walking into the elevator with a group of men. Again, my gut tightens when the doors close, and she's out of my sight. Knowing she's alone with them only adds to my tension. Until I can secure a date, she's at risk.

I step up to the counter to check-in, and the hotel manager greets me. She asks, "Brody Andrews?"

"Affirmative."

She smiles as she walks to the computer and types in my name. "Jeff said to enjoy yourself. You've earned some R&R."

She gives me a room key and a VIP card. "Your ticket to the dinner show is waiting for you." She points the direction, "Tell the hostess who you are, and she'll show you to your seat."

"Thanks," I tell her, then turn for the elevator. There's a crowd of people waiting, so I hit the stairs, taking them three at a time. When I enter the hallway, I glimpse Lizzy rounding the corner and lengthen my stride, hoping to have enough time to catch up before she enters her room. I want her to at least see my badass coming down the hallway, so she'll think about me while she prepares for the evening.

But when I round the corner, she steps into her room —the heavy sound of her door closing echoes down the empty corridor.

Damn. Nothing to do now but wait for her to go down to the show. Going into my room, I toss my rucksack on the bed, then stretch out to nap.

...

The bang of a heavy door closing wakes me.

Lizzy! She's on the move.

**CHAPTER**
# FIVE

*Lizzy*

---

At the restaurant entrance, I confirm my reservation with the hostess, then follow her to the table in the middle of the club. Two couples are already seated, so I take one of the two empty seats and introduce myself.

"Hi, I'm Lizzy."

"Hi Lizzy, I'm Karolina; this is my husband, Frank, my friend Debbie and her husband, Jay."

"Nice to meet you."

The cocktail waitress stops by, and I order a

Sangria Margarita. When I turn my attention back, the four friends talk about work and how the boss mistreats the women. I listen politely for a few minutes and then decide to visit the ladies' room before the show starts. As I stand, I ask for directions. "Excuse me, which way is the ladies' room?"

Debbie glances my way, points behind me, and then the friends laugh at something Karolina said. When I turn to step in the direction, Debbie indicated, I crash into a wall that utters, "Oomph!" And I'm knocked off balance.

Before I can step to keep from falling backward onto the table, warm, strong hands grasp my arms and quickly gain control of my whole body. Gently guiding me down into my chair while a deep, smooth tone apologizes, "Excuse me. I thought you were sitting down, not leaving."

I stare up at the wall, dumbfounded, and the wall stares back, amused.

Solid. Hard. Massive. Handsome as hell. Scary as fuck.

My breath vanishes, my heart races, and my entire body tingles!

"Are you okay?" The beautiful deep tone asks.

The man is too fucking magnificent!

I close my eyes and nod, overwhelmed by his brawn and beauty.

"Did I knock the breath out of you?" He asks, concerned. His words caress my mind while his hands softly, seductively caress my shoulders.

Physically unable to answer, I shake my head. He squats down in front of me to get a closer look.

His musk is overwhelming, intoxicating, all man, and I feel lightheaded. His fingers firmly squeeze my shoulders while his thumbs softly stroke my skin. The tingling created by his touch is electric.

Then he asks so softly only I can hear him. "Are you sure you're okay?"

I can feel his eyes searching my face, analyzing my response, and my eyes can't resist. I look into his.

They are a deep green shade, framed by long dark lashes, and my mouth literally waters. I blush furiously under his scrutiny, but I manage to whisper, "I'm fine."

The wall smiles, and I melt completely.

## Brody

Christ. She's more gorgeous than I thought. Her eyes, her smile, her shyness. Being a Navy SEAL, I'm trained to control my response in any situation, but it's damn hard right now to play it cool with her. That dress is sexy as fuck, and my cock is rock hard.

But I saw fear flash in her eyes, and until I can identify why, I have to play it cool. I don't want to ruin any chance I might have by being too aggressive.

The lights dim as the show begins. A waitress arrives carrying a drink. As I rise, her eyes grow bigger and bigger until I'm towering over her. I see the familiar look of awe on her face as I take the drink from her. "Bring me a Michelob and put this one on my tab."

She nods and walks away.

I turn to Lizzy, lean down as I hand her the drink, and whisper, "Least I can do to apologize is buy your drink. I'm B.A., by the way."

She carefully takes the drink and answers. "Thanks. I'm Lizzy."

The emcee begins the Lost Boys' story narrative, so I pull out the vacant chair and sit. The positioning is less than ideal. I'm too far forward to converse with Lizzy. When the first joke is cracked, the room laughs, and I cast a quick glance over my shoulder. Lizzy is watching me and blushes again when our eyes connect. She reaches for her drink and takes a long hit off of it. I look back at the stage and appreciate my position now, knowing I'm close enough to influence her but not intimidate her.

The cocktail waitress brings my beer, and I stretch my leg out to pull a tip from my pocket. When I lay it on the tray, I tell her. "Bring us another two drinks with our meal." She nods and walks away.

Lizzy opens her mouth to protest, but the whole transaction is over before she can speak. I give her a wink, tap my bottle on her glass, and raise it slowly, waiting on her to accept the toast.

When she takes her drink, she lifts it in silent salute, then brings it to her perfect pouty mouth. My eyes are glued on those puckered lips, and my cock can't wait to feel them suck him like she's sucking that straw. She smiles when she finishes, and I know my thoughts are busted. I grin, raise my bottle to my lips, and let her enjoy the vision too.

The room explodes with laughter, and we smile at each other before I turn my attention back to the stage.

# CHAPTER
# SIX

**Lizzy**

———

That smile. That wink. I stare blatantly at the profile of this wall of a man named B.A. He is a fine specimen of manliness. Although he is enormous and definitely intimidating, my first reaction was wrong. His eyes aren't mean; they are just super serious. They bore into your soul, asking if you have secrets. I bite my straw and take a sip of my free drink. I wonder what his secrets are.

He laughs easily, enjoying the show. His eyes crinkle, and there's a cute dimple in his cheek.

Every time he flexes his arm to lift his beer to those sculpted lips, his muscles pop out. His Adam's apple slides up and down as he swallows. I've never dated a man who had muscles this big or had a pronounced Adam's apple like his. I smirk at that unusual thought and take another sip. *I wonder what it would be like to have an alpha male make mad, passionate love to you. It would be sensory overload!* I suck hard on my straw, draining my drink. The sound of sucking air gets his attention, and he glances back at me.

Totally tipsy, I swing my leg over to cross my legs as I set the empty glass on the table. His eyes drop to the movement and linger, looking at my hemline. Knowing I'm bare down there, his intense gaze makes me both nervous and excited, and the booze makes me daring. *What would a man like him do if I was his girl and I teased him right now by spreading my legs invitingly? Would he ignore the temptation because we're in public, or would he discretely slide his hand between my legs, then insert his finger to test my wetness? I bet he would check my status.* My leg starts to pump up and down with that thought, satisfying the tickle growing down there.

He looks up at my face and catches the

fantasy playing on it. The look on his face shifts in a fraction of a second from a man enjoying a comedy at a dinner show to a man who would fuck my brains out given the opportunity, and I would beg him for more.

My breath hitches in my throat, and my heart stops beating. This man is nothing like the "decent" men I'm used to dating. He pushes my panic button in a way I've never felt before. But not in a scary I'm-afraid-he-will-hurt-me kind of way, but rather, in a dangerous, I'm-never-going-to-look-at-other-men-again sort of way. My whole body is tingling. The look on his face is barely concealed desire, and I bite my lip to keep from coming unglued.

---

**Brody**

---

*Fucking hell! Woman! Don't tease my ass so blatantly. I could fuck that look into tomorrow.*

Out of the corner of my eye, I see the waiter with our food. Thankful for the distraction, I lean back in my seat to gain control of myself as I stare at Lizzy.

*Lucky for you, babe, our food is here because I'm hungry and ready to eat.*

Her eyes stare back, intimated.

The waiter steps between us, blocking my view and sets the entree on the table in front of her. "Madam," he says in a fake accent. "Your Prime Rib is cooked medium as requested."

I hear her take a deep breath, then comment. "Mmmm, it smells delicious."

The sweet sound of her voice keeps my dick hard. I drain my beer, needing to get my shit together.

The waiter snaps his fingers, and his helper passes him another entree. This one has twice the food as her serving had, and he sets the loaded platter in front of me.

*Jeff. Always taking care of me.*

The waiter snaps his fingers again and is handed Lizzy's second Sangria Margarita and two beers for me. When he turns to leave, he pats me on the shoulder and says respectfully, "Thank you for your service. It's on the house."

I offer my hand, and he shakes it. When he walks away, I can see Lizzy again. Her expression makes me chuckle. She is staring at my platter overflowing with food, wearing an astonished look on her face. Her pouty mouth is hanging open, and the thought of filling it with my manhood cancels my deflating dick, and it begins to grow again.

*I guess I will have to deal with her effect on me. There are things you can control and things you can't.*

Knowing she will watch me consume my meal for no reason other than being curious to see if I can finish it all, I pick up my knife and fork to give her a taste of who I am and what she can expect from me. I gently but firmly slice into the tender steak, then stroke steadily back and forth. The rare meat oozes its juice onto the plate, rolling off the knife, unfolding onto the platter, splaying, laid bare, waiting for me to stab it. I poke it with my fork, then push it around to soak up the juice. When I lean toward it and lift it to my open mouth, I pause in midair. Waiting for her eyes to connect with mine, I see the effect of my seduction sitting on her face, and when our eyes connect, I give her my sexy as fuck boyish grin to tease her further and state. "I burn a lot of calories."

She blushes again, busted, and looks down at her plate. I'm not sure if she turned red because she was gawking or because she got the innuendo, but either way, her ability to blush like that makes me want to see how flushed she becomes when she's really tuned up and turned on. I smirk, not taking my eyes off her pretty face. I insert the bite into my mouth and savor the flavor. "Umm, delicious! Soft, juicy, perfection."

Lizzy, pretending she's ignoring me, takes her dinnerware and slices her steak. I know I have her when she begins to smirk as she strokes the meat back and forth. Yup, I stab my steak and slice another piece. She may be shy now, but I'm betting the right man will make her a minx. I lift the delicate part to my lips, smirking, knowing I will be the right man.

# CHAPTER SEVEN

*Lizzy*

---

Sitting here sipping my drink, I'm only half-listening to the show. The actors kicked it up a notch, allowing the audience to enjoy their meal, and I managed to eat most of mine, but this hunk of a man sitting beside me totally captured my imagination. Sure, I laugh when the audience laughs, but I only pretend to be paying attention. There is something about the way he handles his fork and knife that keeps the tingling sensation swirling around down there, fully engaged. I'm hot and wet! He cuts his eyes at me, and I quickly lower mine to stir my drink. If those eyes connect again, zapping my aroused erogenous zones, I will hand this stranger my room key.

A voice behind me says, "Excuse me, may I collect your plate?" The waiter appears to clear the dishes away. He leans in on my right side to remove my plate.

"Yes, thank you," I answer as I turn to look at him. Thankful for the distraction.

"Dessert will be served next. Would you like a cup of coffee with it?" He asks politely.

"No, thank you."

As he steps back, I hear B.A. say, "Would you like another drink instead?"

My heart nearly stops in my chest. His voice is close! Like, super close. My eyes drift to the left. He has pulled his chair next to mine. His aroma hits me again, and damn, he smells good. My eyes drift to his lap to see all the bulges under his jeans. I try hard not to flush at the thought of his cock being close enough to touch.

Dear Lord, I'm a hot mess. I lift my drink. "Thank you, but no, I'm good."

He chuckles, "You do realize your glass is empty again?"

I blink and focus on it. "Oh, so it is."

Embarrassed, I laugh, and my eyes seize on my lapse of control to find his. The intensity in his dark green gaze makes my heart flip over, and I want to stare into them.

He smiles, and his look softens, but the intensity remains the same, making me bite my bottom lip.

"Are you enjoying the show?" He asks.

The question is a reasonable one to ask. But it feels more like he's asking if I'm into him.

"Yes, I am," slips out, "Very much so."

He grins, "I am too."

Oh my! That grin is so cute! He's adorable.

The people around us laugh at something happening on the stage, but we grin at each other.

Then the waiter returns with our desserts. B.A. raises his eyebrows and asks, "You sure you don't need a drink to wash that cake down?"

"Are you afraid I'm going to choke?" I flirt.

He chuckles, "Well if you do, I know the Heimlich maneuver."

Dear Lord, the thought of his arms wrapped around me, crushing my body against his, makes my legs weak and my pussy even wetter.

Can I fake choking? I smile at him, and his eyes tell me he knows what I am thinking.

He looks down at his chest, then retrieves his phone from the front pocket. He stares at it for just a second, then begins to rise. "Excuse me." He tells me, then turns and walks away.

Watching his confident posture disappear, I marvel at what a perfect ass he has. But when he exits the restaurant, the excited breath that I held exhales in a long sigh.

*Just my fucking luck.* I roll my eyes.

Hopeful he's coming back, I glance over more than a few times in the first five minutes, but after that, I realize he's not returning.

Disappointment settles over me, and my only consolation is that he turned toward the hotel area, not out the exit. Maybe he'll be in the bar later.

---

**Brody**

---

Damn, I hate to leave Lizzy. I was starting to gain her trust. But I must answer when duty calls.

Once outside the restaurant, I read the text alert from my unit commander.

> B.A. Congrats. I received notification that your RFO to OCS has been accepted. Your official orders will follow, but I wanted to be the first to offer my congratulations. Welcome to the elite of the elite.

> Fucking A! Thanks for the heads up, Boss.

Grinning, I lower my phone, then unable to contain my excitement, I let out a "Hooyah!" Everyone turns to stare at me, but I don't care. This is excellent news! I text John.

> John, great news! My request for Officer Candidate School has been accepted. Details to follow.

> Congratulations, Little Brother! So proud of you. You deserve it! Are you dancing the night away with Lizzy?

> WORKING ON IT.

> *I didn't tell Tara where you went. Didn't want her asking questions and wanting status updates.*

I laugh at that.

> Good call. Out here.

> *See you Sunday.*

When I turn to head back into the dinner theater, Jeff rounds the corner. He throws his hand up and waves. "Did I hear a hooyah?"

I grin. "Yes, sir! You sure did." I walk to him with my hand outstretched. He clasps it firmly and pumps it.

"Good to see you, Brody."

"You too."

"So, you've gotten good news?"

"Yes, my application for OCS has been accepted."

"That's awesome news! Congratulations!" He pumps my hand again. "When do you leave?"

"I don't know the details yet, just that I'm in."

"Well, this calls for a celebration! Come on," he throws his arm around my shoulder. "Let's go to the bar and toast this amazing news."

I don't want to leave Lizzy behind, but my allegiance to Jeff is without question, so I follow along. Jeff and I shoot the shit on the ride up, catching up on the general details of where I was stationed and how long I've been back.

The elevator arrives, and we exit. The bouncer greets him and is introduced as Damien. Crockett tells him our history and that he is to have my back if I get into a confrontation. We laugh and shake hands. Then I follow Jeff into the bar. Several people shout his name as we head toward the VIP area, and he throws his hand up in acknowledgment. His missions have made him a local legend. When we slide into his booth, a waitress is already there to take our order. She looks at me, "What will you have, cutie?"

I laugh. Cutie. I haven't been called that since grade school. "Bud in a bottle."

"You sure you don't want a frosted mug?"

I laugh again, "Nope. If a fight breaks out, I'll have a weapon."

She laughs, "I should have known you were a SEAL. Coming right up." She spins around and walks off.

I turn to Jeff. "Before I start entertaining you

with war stories, what have you been up to?" I grin at him.

"Nothing good, but that's about to change."

"Let's hear it."

The waitress returns with a bucket of beer. Jeff slides one to me, then lifts one. "First, a toast to your acceptance into the elite of the elite. Hooyah!"

"Hooyah!" I lift the beer, drain it, and then slam the bottle down onto the table simultaneously with Jeff.

He laughs. "Either I'm getting slower, or you're getting better." He slides the next beer over. "I wanted to speak to you about a special project I've been working on. It seems there is a need right here at home for our skills."

"Really?" I lean in.

"A few months ago, I was approached by a family whose son and his girlfriend had been taken hostage while on a mission trip. Long story short, they hired me to put together an extraction team. We went in, did a snatch-and-grab, and brought them both home safely. Word has spread, and I've had multiple missions requested, so I'm assembling a team of special operators." He stops and stares at me.

I rock back in my seat. "And you were going to ask me to join you?"

"Affirmative." He opens two more beers and pushes one to me. "But if you're going to become an officer, you'll have to tact on more years and another tour.

I take the bottle and tip it up. "It will, but I like options. Tell me more."

## CHAPTER
# EIGHT

*Lizzy*

---

As soon as the show is over, I exchange pleasantries with Karolina, Debbie, and their men, agreeing it was terrific and worth every penny paid, then head straight for the elevator. Standing with the crowd, waiting to go up to the bar, my phone vibrates. It's Tara.

> Are you dancing yet?

> GOING UP TO THE BAR NOW.

> *OK. HAVE FUN. DANCE THE NIGHT AWAY.*

> *I FULLY INTEND TO.*

> *PROMISE ME. YOU WILL DANCE WITH A DUDE THAT IS NOT DECENT IN YOUR BOOK. ;)*

I smile at my phone, hoping B.A. is in the bar.

> I will.

When the elevator doors open, the music is loud. My heart starts to race. I am so ready for a night of fun. I prove my age, get my hand stamped, then walk in. The joint is jumping. Quickly scanning the area for B.A., I'm disappointed I don't see him, but it is possible I missed him.

The dance floor is crowded, and so are the tables and booths surrounding it. Heading across the room to the bar, I walk around the edge of the dancers, still on the lookout, but no luck spotting him. When I arrive, the patrons waiting for their drinks are five deep, and I know because I'm short, I have to get closer to be seen and served, so I weave in and out of the crowd until I'm behind the second row. The bartender spots me as he hands two drinks to the couple in front of me. When they turn to leave, I slide into their space. He smiles as he leans toward me. I shout, "Sangria Margarita, please." He nods his acknowledgment and begins to make it.

Two guys seated at the bar turn to check me out. I smile, and they lean away from each other, inviting me to step between them. They are dressed in suits with their shirt collars unbuttoned and their ties loosened. *Lawyers.*

They lean back in and shout simultaneously when I take the position offered.

"Hi, I'm Greg."

"Hi, I'm Matt."

Then they glare at each other. Remembering the "dibs" call from earlier, I laugh. "Hi," I tell them, "I'm Lizzy."

The bartender slides my drink to me, and Matt tells him. "Put that on my tab."

I smile at the bartender, firmly telling him, "I got this." Then I slide my hand inside the V-neck of my dress and pull my credit card from under my bra strap.

The bartender grins as he reaches for the card. "Yes, ma'am."

"It guarantees I buy my own drinks." I wink at him, and we all laugh.

When he returns my card with my drink, I carefully return it to its safe place.

Matt's eyes are glued to my tits, and when I pull my hand out, he says with a grin, "I hope you drink a lot."

I laugh as I pull my drink to me and take a sip. "Are you two attending the conference?"

"We are," Greg answers.

"Are you from here?" I ask.

Matt answers, "No, we flew in from the coast."

"Are you from here?" Greg asks.

"Just visiting for the weekend too."

Greg looks around. "You with someone?"

I glance at the mirror, trying to bide time while thinking of how to answer that. I don't want them to know I'm here alone, so I answer. "I'm waiting on someone."

Greg and Matt exchange a look over my head. They don't believe me. I lift my drink to my lips and take a sip.

Matt leans toward me and asks if I want to dance. He smells good, but not as good as B.A.

*Am I going to compare everyone from now on to him? That's problematic.*

---

## Brody

---

It is all I can do to focus on Jeff's project. Lizzy walked into the bar about 15 minutes ago, looking absolutely breathtaking in her dress and heels. Her voluptuous body made my dick grow hard again. But she disappeared into the crowd at the bar, and I lost sight of her.

"Brody, I'd love to have you join my team. I'd compensate you well for your time. You'll get a cut of the contract when you're on a mission. When you're not on a mission, you'll be required to train regularly, of course, and you'll have a set salary that we can discuss later. Besides that, you'll have all the free time you want."

I lift my beer and take a draw. "Who's the money man backing you?"

"His name is Aurei Moore. He's a venture

capitalist, former Army Aviator, and Apache pilot. We go way back."

"Do you have training facilities?"

"Yes, Aurei bought a ranch outside of Vegas."

"Vegas, huh?" I grin.

"Yeah. It's definitely a perk." He grins too.

"Who else have you recruited?"

He gives me a quick rundown of the special operators who have signed on.

"Sounds like an impressive group."

"They are. Does it sound like something you'd be interested in?" He lifts his brew and takes a draw.

"You have given me something to think about. I love what I do, but I'll consider it."

"Fair enough." He says and sits back in his seat.

I look at the dance floor and glimpse Lizzy moving and grooving among the other dancers. She's graceful and gorgeous. My eyes feast on her beauty, and I feel a hunger for her growing in the pit of my stomach.

Jeff asks, "So, tell me about your last mission?"

I open my mouth to begin my accounting of what went down when I see the dude Lizzy's dancing with, and my words vanish. It irks me, knowing he is enjoying her attention. I shift in my seat and reach for another beer. If I've got to endure watching her with someone else, I will need more alcohol.

Jeff turns his head, looking in the same direction. He laughs, "I'm betting that's *Miss* Lizzy Mayer out there dancing with another man from the look on your face."

"Yes" is the only word I say before I drain my beer. Lizzy's sensual moves stir that something inside my gut and groin that no one else has ever awakened before, and I watch her maneuvering just out of reach of the dude she's dancing with. I begin recounting my mission to Jeff with my eyes glued on her.

I'm just getting to the first encounter with the insurgents when I realize another man has joined them. He slides up behind Lizzy, cutting her retreat from the first dude, but she isn't aware yet. The first dude reaches for her, and as she tries to dance away, she dances right into the second dude. I sense this isn't the first time they have done this. I sit up in my chair and watch, concerned for her. Pinned between them, she stops dancing and looks for a way out. When the first dude grabs her arm, jerking her body against his, and the second dude prepares to grind her from behind, I stand up. My jaw sets and I utter between clenched teeth, "Later, Jeff."

"Let me know if you need my help. I'll send my boys over there."

"I got this," I tell him, walking onto the dance floor. As I weave my way to Lizzy, I keep my cool by repeating, 'She's not my girl. She's not my girl.' But when I see her struggling to push him away, I lose it. 'She's not my girl ... yet.'

# CHAPTER NINE

*Lizzy*

---

Matt's dancing has turned to full-on groping. His hand squeezes the piss out of my tit, and now Greg has joined in my assault. He has grabbed a handful of my ass.

"Let me go," I yell, but they are too drunk to care. I try to shove Matt as hard as possible, but he only laughs at me. Then Greg grabs a handful of my hair, stopping me in my tracks.

"Don't fight us, little girl. We are going to make all your dreams come true."

My eyes flare with fright, and Matt laughs, thinking Greg's words have scared me, but it's not that. Through the dancers, I spot B.A. His frown and the intensity on his face are mean as hell! When B.A. clears the last dancer between us, he stops short. He doesn't say anything to me. He stares into my eyes with those beautiful green eyes framed by those long dark lashes. Knowing I will be rescued, relief floods my body, and I take a deep breath. B.A. smiles at me, and I melt with the gentleness I see on his face.

Then the ruthless look returns, and he steps up, staring into Greg's eyes while he grabs Matt's shoulder and spins him around. Then he turns a vicious face on them that says, 'back the fuck off, boys, or I'll annihilate you,' and I swear I hear him growl.

Greg immediately releases my ass, and I feel him back away, but Matt is too drunk to give it up without talking smack. "Take a hike, hero. We found her first."

B.A. bows up and towers over us, and I realize he isn't the kind of man who ever backs down. Not wanting a fight to break out, I step around Matt and walk up to B.A. I put my hand on his chest, and his eyes find mine. The connection between us is electric. He ignores Matt, who is still mouthing off and opens his arms to me. I slide into them, and my heart stops beating as he lowers his perfectly sculpted lips to mine. I stop breathing altogether when he whispers, "Forgive me, Lizzy, but ...."

Then his lips touch mine, and my knees buckle with the gentleness of his touch, the sweetness of his taste, and the intoxication of his alpha maleness. His response to my weakness is to pull me tight against his body. I part my teeth for him, and he inserts his tongue, kissing me deeply and completely. My entire being tunes into his dominance, shutting out everything else. The only two people in the world are him and me.

When I cling to him, he relaxes and lets his tongue explore my mouth, knowing he owns me. When my arms move up his chest to embrace his neck, his hands respond by sliding to the small of my back and crushing my body against his. His kiss becomes more passionate, and I feel like I'm drowning in my desire, wanting more of him to own more of me. I will never find another man who can kiss me so completely.

When he finally lifts his mouth off mine, I

don't know how long we have kissed, but a new song is playing. I open my eyes and stare into his. He smiles that cute boyish grin, and I know he knows that I am not only hot and horny for him but that he is in total control.

"I think I scared them off." He says as his hands rest on my waist.

I glance around. Matt and Greg are nowhere in sight. "It would appear that way." I look back up at him. "Thank you."

"You're welcome." B. A. smiles gently down at me. "I'm glad I realized you were ... uncomfortable." He says softly.

"I'm glad you did too." Then I look back at the bar and see Matt and Greg glaring at us. A chill runs down my spine when I realize how badly that could have turned out if B.A. hadn't intervened.

---

## Brody

---

My dick is so hard it hurts. Staring down at Lizzy

with the taste of her still in my mouth, it's hard not to retake control of her. My hands refuse to let her go wanting to pull her back into my embrace. She's looking over at the bar. I follow her gaze and see the two men I scared off glaring at us.

*Motherfuckers! I should beat their ass for them.*

Lizzy begins to tremble. I look down at her sweet face and see the realization of what could have happened to her dawn on her. My arm slides around her waist again, and I pull her tight to me. When her body presses against mine, she lays her face against my chest. My arm tightens, and her trembling stops. I lean over and ask, "What say you and I get out of here and get some fresh air?"

She nods.

Keeping her safe, I lead her through the dancers to the elevator. While we wait on it to arrive, I call the bouncer over. Without releasing Lizzy, I give him a brief description of what went down and who they are. "Better keep your eyes on those two. They are up to no good."

He nods, pulls his radio out, and retakes his post.

Lizzy squeezes me tight, and I give her shoulder a reassuring squeeze.

When the elevator arrives, we board it with a crowd of others and ride silently to the lobby. When the doors open, she releases me and walks out first. I follow, and when we enter the lobby, she hesitates.

Knowing I'm not letting her go again, I walk up to her, throw my arm around her shoulders and lead her out the front door. She follows willingly, and when she slides her arm around my waist, I know she trusts me. Leading her away from the hotel, I take her down the sidewalk to stroll past the restaurants. When we passed two establishments, we come upon a Dairy Queen, and I ask her, "Want some ice cream?"

She looks up at me and says with a sweet smile. "Sure."

I open the door for her, and she walks in. She waits for me to join her, but she doesn't slide back into my embrace. We walk up to the counter, and I ask her. "Do you have a favorite?"

"Of course," she laughs. "A Hot Fudge Sunday, please." The sound is beautiful, and I see the confident woman I saw at my brother's house return.

I approach the counter and order hers with a vanilla cone for myself. She teases me. "Vanilla is boring."

I chuckle. "That's not necessarily true. All flavors begin with vanilla. Therefore, vanilla is the foundation for the rest of the flavors because it's pure."

She squints her eyes and looks at me with new appreciation. I chuckle to myself. *Nope, I'm not just brawn; I've got a brain too.*

After I pay, we are given a number, and I ask Lizzy where she would like to sit. "Outside."

I bow slightly and wave my hand, "After you."

She smiles, twirls around, and twitches her cute little ass to a place on the patio that's secluded. When she chooses a chair, she reaches for it, but I lean over her, intercept her hand, and pull her chair back for her to sit. Her smile tells me manners are important to her, and I scored more brownie points.

# CHAPTER
# TEN

*Lizzy*

———

B.A. pulls the chair out across from me, but before he can sit, our ice cream order is called. Watching him walk back to the counter, I study him. *Fuck! He's unbelievably good-looking and totally swoon-worthy, and his kiss was velvety and sensuous!*

He takes my cup and his cone, then heads back to me. Unable to resist, he lifts his ice cream to his mouth, sticks his tongue out, and drags a nice long lick from bottom to top. Instantly, I tingle, knowing I want that tongue doing that to my pussy. I look down, trying not to give my thoughts and feelings away. I don't want him to get the wrong idea about the kind of girl I am after what just happened to me. I was careless, but I'm not easy.

I shudder again, thinking about what could have happened. Greg and Matt could have …. Stop! Don't let those horrible thoughts get inside your head. Thank God B.A. is the kind of man willing to take action and step up to defend someone when they need it.

I look up at him and smile. He's the kind of man women like me dream of. Suddenly, the truth of that thought clears the fog of desire from my mind. Men like him don't notice women like me, much less hookup. He's too awesome, and I'm nothing special. I feel the air leave my chest. The all-too-familiar depression fills the pit of my stomach. He's not flirting with me! He's feeling sorry for me! For crying out loud, he apologized before he kissed me! His kiss was just to get rid of Greg and Matt without a fight. His attention is because he looks at me as a victim, rescuing me from the bad guys. I lower my head and cover my face. I moan softly, "I'm so fucking stupid!"

"You aren't stupid. They are." He says it so matter-of-factly I look at him.

He thinks I'm talking about Greg and Matt, not myself. I smirk. He's definitely a hero. I shake my head. "I'm the one who is stupid."

"Hey, let that go. Push it out of your mind," B.A. says. "Those dudes need their asses kicked. Later on, I might return and handle that myself." Sliding my ice cream cup to me, he adds. "Eat your ice cream. You'll feel better."

He sticks his damn mouthwatering tongue out and licks his cone again, and my pussy soaks itself. I can't deny wanting him, even if he doesn't want me. Just being with him makes me feel better. I pull the ice cream to me and begin to eat it.

We sit in silence while I take my time. Not wanting to say goodbye to B.A., I study my cup while slowly spooning the sweet treat past my lips, laying it on my tongue, and savoring the flavor. He's right. The ice cream makes me feel better.

About halfway through, I realize every time I open my lips, his eyes are locked onto them. I chance a glance up and find them hooded with desire.

God, I blush; I'll take whatever he's offering, even if it's only a blow job. I lick my lips, and he shifts in his seat.

Then when I lock eyes with him, he smirks, not hiding the look of desire. Maybe he will give me a sympathy fuck.

He bites his cone. His eyes tease me, "Feeling better?"

"Yes," I smile back. "Thanks."

"No problem." He answers before he shoves the remainder of the cone in his mouth.

I may not be anything special any other night of the week, but tonight I am. Tonight, I was a maiden in distress, and my knight in shining armor came to my rescue. Nothing wrong with thanking him for his service. I smirk again — nothing wrong at all with that.

---

**Brody**

---

I sit back in my seat, stretch my legs out in front, and ease the pressure of my pants on my erection. Watching the sensual way Lizzy eats her ice cream has my cock throbbing with the need to be consumed like that. Her pouty lips are puckered perfection, and the way her mouth gently sucks the spoon before she rolls it across her tongue, then slides it out, and starts the seduction again, is driving my mind mad with thoughts of how wild her blow jobs must be. By the time she's taken the last bite, I've formulated my plan on how I'm going to take her back to her room and pound her sweet little pussy into a mound of moaning muscle and make her mine.

"Lizzy?"

"Yes?" She looks up at me with those big beautiful eyes.

"Would you like to go back to the bar and dance the night away with me?"

She squints suspiciously, then she asks, "Why?"

I frown at her. "Why?"

"Yes, why? Do *you* want to dance?"

Christ Almighty! I can't answer that truthfully. Hell no! I want to take you to bed and fuck your brains out, but I can't say that.

I decide to answer semi-truthfully and diplomatically. "Only if you do." I wait for her answer, but she's silent, so I gamble and explain further. "If you want to dance, I'll take you back to the bar and dance all night with you. Not because I particularly like to dance, and not because you need me to be safe, but because the way your beautiful body moves to the music promises a night spent in your bed will be a night spent without sleep, and I'm hoping one thing will lead to the other." I grin at her, then wink.

She blushes a deep, perfect shade of hotness. I stand up, take the ice cream cup from the table, and walk to the trash receptacle to dispose of it. When I turn back, she has followed me, and I nearly knock her down again. Reaching out, I grab her shoulders to stabilize her. We stare at each other for what feels like forever, then she whispers, "You had me at 'Oomph.'" Her shy smile makes my heart thump as hard as my dick, then she steps into my arms and offers her perfect pouty lips.

# CHAPTER
# ELEVEN

*Lizzy*

---

B.A.'s deep green eyes close as he lowers his face to mine, and his sculpted lips part just before they kiss me. His soft lips caress mine before he slips his tongue inside.

Umm, the taste of him is better than any succulent dessert I've ever eaten, and my mouth waters with his deliciousness. His hands slide around my waist, pulling me roughly, hungrily, against the wall of his body.

He takes his time and explores my mouth, and I let him. His breath, as it flows gently across my cheeks, makes me aware that my essence is tuned into his and enhances the closeness of the moment. His fingers flex, kneading my back to a rhythm that promises his thrusting tempo will have me shivering with more than one orgasm. His tongue, as it travels in and out, around and around, promises he knows what he's doing, and I will be begging him to give me everything he has later tonight. But it's the power in his kiss that speaks to my soul on a much deeper level than anyone I've ever been with before. He is a man I will need, and that scares me.

When he finally stops kissing me, he cups my face, and his eyes take possession of mine. I stare into his completely owned, and they assure me I am beautiful, memorable, and worthy of a man like him.

Without another word, he laces our fingers together, and I feel bonded to him. He leads me back to the hotel in silence, and for the first time in my life, I don't feel the need to know anything about the man I'm giving myself to. He is a hero, and that is enough.

---

## **Brody**

---

Walking with Lizzy back to the hotel, feeling her small, soft hand in mine, trusting me without knowing me, is nothing short of exhilarating. I look down at her, and my heart softens with her smile.

When we enter the lobby, Jeff is standing there, surrounded by a small group of men. He flags me down, and Lizzy and I walk over. He steps away from the group to speak to us. He looks at Lizzy and smiles but doesn't let on he knows anything about her; then he looks at me with an intensity that says introductions will have to wait. His voice is stern, business-like, and I see the legend in action. "B.A., I just received a call. A friend of mine needs my services."

I nod toward the group of men, "These guys part of your team?"

"Yeah, we're assembling for a briefing before we fly down." He sticks his hand out. "We'll catch up later."

"No worries, brother. It was good seeing

you." I clasp it, then give him a bro hug, "Good luck. Hope the mission is successful."

He nods, "It will be."

I look the group over as he returns to them. There are four men. Three of which I know. They are former Bravo One team members and served with Crockett. The other I don't recognize. They briefly give me eye contact, then focus on Crockett. He starts to talk as soon as he returns.

I look down at Lizzy. Her eyes are as big as saucers, but she doesn't say anything. I take her little hand in mine again, and we walk to the elevator to wait. When it arrives and the doors open, the two douchebags who worked on having a threesome on the dance floor with Lizzy have found a willing woman based on the giggling she is doing.

I feel Lizzy tense up, so I put my arm around her shoulder and pull her against my body. She hugs herself tight against me, and her tits press into my ribs. Instantly, my cock is hard again. I close my eyes and savor the moment. I have never had a woman who turns me on with such a simple touch.

"Hey, you!" A man shouts too loud for the space.

I open my eyes to see the dark-haired one has stopped right in front of us and is gawking at Lizzy. I frown at him and clench my teeth.

He slurs, "It's not too late. You can still join in on the fun."

As I raise my hand to block any attempt his stupid drunk punk-ass might try, I growl at him. "Back off."

He glances up at me, but his eyes are glazed. He's more than drunk. He's stoned. "But you'll have to ditch the gorilla. I don't think he will play nice."

The giggling girl smiles at us, "No, I don't think he shares." Then she takes his arm and pulls him away. "Come on, daddy. Mama wants to play."

The three of them stumble off, laughing. I look down at Lizzy, who is still snuggled up against me. She whispers, "Thanks again for being my ...."

I laugh, "Gorilla?"

She laughs too. Then she releases my waist, takes my hand, and we follow the crowd into the waiting elevator. She maneuvers us to the back, then stands in front of me. Her scent wafts up, and she smells like a woman should. Sweet, like flowers. I rest my hands on her shoulders and breathe deep as my thumbs absentmindedly stroke her soft skin. The urge to nip her neck is hard to resist, but I do. The elevator is crowded, which isn't the place for that level of seduction.

When the elevator begins to move, Lizzy leans against me, relaxed. My cock grows again, wanting desperately to touch her skin to skin. I know she can feel it pressing against her ass. "Hmm," slips past my lips when she pushes back. She tilts her head, letting her straight hair fall off her shoulder, exposing her neck to me. My grip tightens, resisting the temptation to at least kiss her there. When she arches her back and rubs her ass against my now hard cock, I lose the battle of wills between discipline and desire. My hand eases into her thick, silky strands at the nape of her neck, and I curl my fingers around them. Controlling her movement, I lean forward and turn her face to kiss, knowing I will hammer her beautiful big ass tonight until she comes again and again for me.

The man at the panel asks, "Everyone going up to the bar?"

I stop my kiss and stare into her eyes. The words "Second floor, please," are on the tip of my tongue, but something about her expression makes me eat them. I see a hint of doubt through her desire, or maybe it's lack of confidence hiding deep inside them, but it gives me pause. I can't push her until I can determine what that look is saying.

She has to be the one who opens up to me. I can't coerce. She has to trust me, and she's more time. I peck her lips and whisper on them, "Let's go dancing."

Her eyes flash that look again, and I wonder if I made a mistake. Then her smile brightens the darkness, and although my cock isn't too happy with my heart, I know it's the right call. She has to want to belong to me before I take her and make her mine. Otherwise, we won't last.

## CHAPTER
# TWELVE

*Lizzy*

---

I smile at B.A. *Wow, you are amazing!*

He releases his grip on my hair, spins me around to face the front, then pulls me tight against him while his thumbs return to stroking my shoulders. How many men would delay their sexual gratification with a willing woman to take her dancing because *she* wants to dance? None that I've ever known.

B.A. takes my hand when the elevator arrives and leads me straight to the dance floor. We weave our way to the center, then he turns to face me, pulls me to him with a force that makes me grunt, catches me with his other hand, and expertly pushes me into a spin, pulls me back into his embrace, then drops me in a dip. He laughs at my shocked face. "Babe, this gorilla's got game."

I laugh out loud with him. To say the man can dance is an understatement. The man can fucking dance is more accurate. Although he is big and bulky, he moves like a cat, graceful and fluid, but the best part of dancing with him is how his eyes devour me. He knows one thing is definitely leading to the other.

His natural confidence, mixed with his desire for me, feels so good to my bruised ego. Fuck all the jackasses in the world. They don't hold a candle to the badasses of the world.

As we move and groove, teasing and tempting each other, I catch the occasional woman dancing around us with envy in her eyes. They would die to be me right now.

I meet their eyes with fight in mine. He isn't the only one who doesn't share.

---

## **Brody**

---

Lizzy! Wow, she's something else. Watching her enjoying the music, dancing carefree, has me wanting her more than I thought possible. But her flirting and teasing me has driven me past the point of no return.

I knew the first time I laid eyes on her she was special, and now that I've met her, I know how special she is. But when I kissed her, I knew for sure that she's *my* someone special.

Each time she dances by, showing me that she's got all the goods to make all my fantasies come true, then stabbing my mind with her wicked eyes that promise she will be brave and daring in her lovemaking, to flashing her beautiful smile that makes my heart feel like it's going to burst, I realize I'm the luckiest man alive because I'm not a liar. Not even to myself. As a behavioral specialist, it's my job to see through the lies and discover the truth. And the truth is, I've fallen for Miss Lizzy Mayer. Now all I have to do is make her fall for me.

The music has been a mixture of current pop

tunes with an occasional country music classic thrown in the mix. So when the perfect song comes on, I take advantage of the opportunity to pierce Lizzy's protective veil and let John Michael Montgomery tell her, "I Can Love You Like That."

At first, we sway together, then I stop and step forcefully into her space, exerting my will into her world. Towering over her, I pinch her chin and tip her perfect face up. When our eyes connect, the intensity of my gaze burns directly from my heart and incinerates all her doubts and insecurities. I bare my soul to her, and before the song is over, she understands that my passion is pure.

When the song ends, I cup her face in my hands and lower my lips to hers. Releasing the fire burning inside, I consume her. When her arms wrap themselves around my neck, and she clings to me without reservation, I know I have won. She is mine.

When I finally pull away, my cock demands I consummate her capitulation. My mind and heart are in complete agreement. Without asking, I take her hand and head for the elevator. I can feel her trotting to keep up, but the driving force burning inside me won't slow down. I've waited for her all my life. When I kissed my first girlfriend, I knew she wasn't the one and that I would know when I located my soulmate. Lizzy is that person.

When we reach the elevator, Damien, the bouncer, is back on point. He takes one look at my face, glances at Lizzy, then steers us to Jeff's private elevator. He hits the button, and the door opens. Without breaking my stride, I drag Lizzy inside, and before the door has closed completely, I have her pinned against the back wall.

The silence shouts privacy.

The elevator begins to move.

I bury my face in the nape of her neck and breathe in her essence.

*Fuck, she smells good.*

My hips pin her while my hands slide down her arms to grasp her hands. Lifting them over her head, wanting her submissive, my lips attack hers.

Her mouth opens wide, and when I thrust my tongue inside, she sucks it hard, then rolls it around hers. The vision of the sexy way she ate ice cream appears, and my sack fills with semen as she demonstrates her skills.

Ding. The elevator passes the first floor going down. Then it stops. We both freeze, wondering if the doors will open and we will have to stop and wait until we reach the room.

I turn my ear to the door and listen.

The only sound is the sound of our heavy breath refusing to be held.

No noise. Complete silence.

I grin. *Damien is a team player.*

I look back at Lizzy. Her big, brown eyes look like liquid caramel. Her lids hang heavy with lust.

I pull her arms up, stretching her, and grind my hard cock against her hips. I'm going to ram it so deep inside her she will forget all about the other cocks before mine. I'm going to own her pussy outright.

I clasp both her hands with one of mine and stare into her eyes. She doesn't blink. Desire, longing, wanting, stare back.

The urge to take her, to fuck her hard and fast, making her mine right now, is so strong I grab her jaw and force her face to mine.

God, she is gorgeous!

I stare into her eyes, searching for her secrets before I fuck her.

*Are there issues? Are there scars? Can I take you and make you mine, now? Or do I need to go slow?*

"Lizzy?"

"Oh, yes, B.A.!" She says in a breathy sigh, and her head tilts, giving me what I want. Control of her body. Her eyes roll back in her head with passion as she closes her eyes. Not shutting me out but savoring the moment. My raging beast takes a deep controlling breath. I know the connection between us is exceptional, and as much as I want to take her and fuck her, I realize she's the kind of woman who deserves a man willing to make love to her, not a man whose first fuck is a wham-bam-thank-you-ma'am selfish act. Her eyes revealed she had had those before.

I slide my hand lightly down her neck, and she squirms. Then I shove it into her cleavage and under her bra. Her big tit fills my hand, and I cup it, then start teasing her nipple. The moan that she emits fills my balls with semen.

I push the fabric down, then lower my lips to it and latch on. Sucking, licking, biting, teasing her. She gasps and moans over and over again, and her passion is so satisfying to hear. Her fingers flex, and her back arches as I take my time, enjoying her passion.

When she starts to writhe, I ease my hand roughly down her dress, and she responds by parting her legs for me.

Again, she says in a breathy sigh that's sexy as fuck, "Oh, yes, B.A!" Then she lifts a leg and hooks it around my hip.

I moan, miserable. Trying to control my lust, but impatient to have her, I release her hands, and with both of mine, I find the hem of her dress and snatch it up over her ass.

*Fuck me! She's not wearing panties!*

I groan, wanting her so fucking bad. I dip my legs, grab a hand full of her big ass, and squeeze her cheeks as I lift her hips to sit on my cock. Greedily, I grind it against her, thankful it's still in my pants.

Her hands claw at my arms, holding on. I shove her dress up over her voluptuous tits. Her bra sits cockeyed. One tit is out; one tit is in. *Mmm*, my mouth waters.

It's a front clasp, and when I unlatch it, they spring free, making me groan again. Unable to resist, I cup them, squeeze them, knead them, then lock my lips onto one perfect tip, suck it hard, and pull my mouth off with a pop, watching it shrink even tighter as the rest of it jiggles.

Then I move to the other one and repeat the tease. Her groan is uninhibited and loud. Arching her back, she offers them to me to devour.

Wanting more of her perfection, my hands move back down to her naked pussy, and I moan against her tit with how wet she is. My fingers stroke her perfection as she sits on my hidden cock. My mouth mauls her breasts, sucking, licking, nipping.

Her breath turns into whimpering pants. Then I ease my fingers inside her, and she moans beautifully for me as her body begins to beg.

A surge of power runs through me as I build her passion. Slowly sinking to my knees, I hold her against the wall until her legs fall over my shoulder. That's when I taste heaven.

*Fuck!*

She shivers as I lick her delicious pussy, inserting my fingers again, and call her g-spot to come for me. Her clit hardens, and her legs begin to quiver. She's about to explode for me when I reach up, massage her tit, tweaking her nipple, and her fingers curl on my head. When she becomes paralyzed at the moment before orgasm, I suck her clit, pinch her nipple hard, and ram my fingers in and out as fast as possible. Her scream is loud and long as her body bucks with contractions, banging the wall.

Pre-cum seeps out of my throbbing cock as it pulsates, wanting to penetrate and pound her pussy, knowing only it can give her the ultimate orgasm, but I make myself wait.

When her orgasm ends, I stand and keep her pinned to the wall, studying her as reality returns to her.

When her eyes flutter open, she smirks a little embarrassed, but I grin, knowing the best one is coming next. I will blow her fucking mind with another orgasm before this one fades away. The second one is always sweeter than the first.

# CHAPTER
# THIRTEEN

*Lizzy*

---

I stare at B.A. and reach for his handsome face, whispering, "Christ Almighty! That was ..." His lips descend on mine again as he gives me a deep, lover's kiss. I can taste my cum on his face. His tongue flicks mine, making my clit tingle, and I can't help the smile that breaks our connection.

He lifts his head and chuckles as his hand moves into my hair. When his fingers curl themselves in the thickness, and he controls my head, I realize he isn't finished with me yet, and my heart starts to race again with glorious anticipation. Then his lips return to my mouth, and his kiss is deep, meaningful, and amazing.

I lose myself in his reality again as his other hand glides lightly over my tits, my abs, my ass, and between my thighs, making my skin very aware of who is in charge. The heightened sensations make my clit super excited, but he doesn't go there. He avoids my diva-ness, and the hunger builds for him as goosebumps break out wherever he touches. My skin literally feels like it's singing.

He pinches my nipple and thumbs the sensitive ridges. Deep inside, past my clit and g-spot, my vagina aches in response. A hunger like I have never known before begins to grow.

My arms wrap themselves around his waist, and I try to pull him against me, but he holds himself away. I start to squirm with the aching need, but he doesn't stop. He keeps kissing and stroking my skin. It's such a sensual seduction.

My head falls back, and "Fuuuuccccckkkkk" falls out of my mouth.

He bites my nipple, and the pain shoots straight to my clit, making my hips jerk. The ache inside doubles down, and I groan, "B.A., please."

He talks with my tit stuck in his mouth, and my nipple bounces happily around, banging on his teeth and tongue. "Please, what, Lizzy?"

Gawd, the vibration from the z's makes me moan again. "Please. You're driving me mad!"

He chuckles, "Not yet."

"Why not," I strain to say.

"We haven't had the talk." He sucks and licks.

"What talk?"

"Condom?"

"I don't have any, do you?"

"No."

I groan my desperation. "Fuck!"

He lifts his head and looks at me. "I'm clean if you are."

"Yes. Yes!" I pant, relieved.

"Are you on birth control?"

"Of course!" I practically shout.

His mouth latches back on my tit, and his tongue starts to dance across my tip. The deep spot begins to throb harder, and I groan, begging. "Pleeaaase!"

"Please, what?" He asks, and I swear he's laughing.

I look down and watch him play. The joy on his face is evident, and my heart melts. "B.A.?" I ask, and he lifts his eyes to mine. "I need you to fuck me!"

He grins that boyish grin that's so dang cute! "But I don't want to fuck you."

I frown as the world stops turning. "What?" My voice sounds pathetic.

"I don't want to fuck you, Lizzy. I want to make love to you."

The sincerity in his voice and the expression on his face are real.

My heart freaks out.

---

**Brody**

---

Boom!

She's mine. It's written all over her face.

Now, to prove it to her. I grin again, take a step back, and unlatch my belt. Her eyes fall to watch. I unbutton, then unzip my jeans. Hook them with my thumbs and push them down off my ass. My cock stands at attention for her.

The look on her face is priceless. I know I'm well endowed, and now, she knows too.

Eager to enter her, I step forward, reach under her arms, and lift her off her feet. She spreads her legs for me, and as I lower her body, my cock tries to slide inside, but she's too tight.

"Ooo," she breathes, frustrated.

I lift her off, and she whimpers, "No, no, no."

I lower her again, and when the head touches her wet slit, she grips my shoulders and grinds it until the tip glides inside.

Fuck! She feels like velvet. "Mmmmm."

She hooks her ankles behind my back. Her hard stiletto heels dig into my butt cheeks as she tries to force my cock further in. Not wanting to rip her, I place my hands on her hips to control the depth of the fuck.

She pumps her wet pussy along my shaft, lubricating it, and my cock inches its way inside.

Her softness gripping it so tight is mind-blowing. When I'm three-quarters in, her lips latch onto mine, and I thrust my tongue in her mouth. Eager for all of my cock, she sucks my tongue hard, and her thrusting becomes manic.

Losing control of her hips, I walk her to the wall to pin her against it, so I can carefully thrust into her, but her manic fucking thrusts my cock to its hilt. My knees nearly buckle with the intense pleasure, and we both groan with the feeling.

*Goddamn, she is heaven.*

She retreats and thrusts herself from one end to the other, and I lean against the wall, arching my back, and let her go.

Every time my cock hits bottom, the tip hits her cervix, and we moan together. No one has ever fucked me so completely.

I swing her around with a growl and thrust into her. The pleasure is so sweet in its intensity it feels like stars exploding.

The sound of our sex grows louder and louder as my heavy breathing combines with the slamming of her body up against the wall. The squishing of our juices, the smacking of our nakedness colliding, and the cries of her mantra, "Yes, Yes, Oh, My God, Yes!"

Picking up speed, moving faster and faster, I pound her tight pussy, ramming inside her.

When she seizes up, holding her breath and

straining against my cock, I pull out to the edge and pause. Her fingertips dig into my back, and unable to wait any longer, I explode into her. Driving deep and spurting into her.

She loses her shit and screams.

# CHAPTER
# FOURTEEN

*Lizzy*

---

Wham!

The forceful spurt of semen blasts my tingling core with such power that I gasp with satisfaction. FINALLY, SOMEONE HAS .... Then the thick cum oozes over it, tickling it, and the whole world vanishes. That one spot is the universe. Then his giant, hard, perfection hammers it, and my mind explodes with rapture.

I scream at the top of my lungs.

"OH."

"MY."

"GOD!"

Over and over again, wave after wave of sweet rapture racks my entire being as B.A. morphs from man to GOD!

My whimpers mingle with his snorts as he takes up into orbit, straight to heaven.

When it's over, I'm unable to hold my head up, weak as a baby, and I meld into his body.

When I open my eyes again, reality returns, and I find he's cradling me like one too. I look into his deep green eyes and find peace, contentment, and love.

"Hey," he smirks. "Welcome back."

I blush and laugh, "Wow! Holy hell!"

He chuckles, pleased, then says, "We've made a mess."

I joke, "*You* made a mess."

His boyish grin is back, then he puckers his lips for a butterfly kiss, and my heart melts. I peck them and seal the deal.

Then he leans away and pins me against the wall, "Hang on."

Crossing his arms, he grabs the hem of his shirt and lifts it up over his head.

My eyes devour the sight of his massive pecs,

eight-pack abs, and tight, flat "V" that points to his cock still buried inside me.

*God, he is beautiful!*

"Use this to catch the evidence." He jokes.

I take it from him as he slowly lowers our bodies until I can stand alone. Then I slide it between my legs as he withdraws his cock, and I cover my vagina with it to catch his cum.

He shuffles a couple of steps backward and kicks his shoes off. Then he hooks his pants with his thumbs, pushes them to the floor, and steps out.

Naked! Butt ass naked. His body is magnificent! The site of his massive perfection stuns me.

His upper body has muscles that bulge on top of muscles. His legs are big, powerful, and straight. And in between is a small waist with washboard abs, holding up a broad, massive chest with pecs that look permanently swole. And his limp cock is bigger than any hard dick I've ever seen.

"Damn, you are a stud," slips out in a whisper as I gawk at him, openly admiring him.

He leans over, retrieves his briefs from his pants, and says, "Since you didn't wear cum catchers, you'll have to wear my briefs under your dress."

"Cum catchers?" I frown.

"Panties. That's their sole purpose."

I laugh, "Obviously, I didn't know that." I cock an eyebrow at his briefs. "I'm not wearing your briefs."

He smiles and brushes away a tress of hair from my cheek. "You are if you don't want everyone to see my cum running down your leg." Then he kneels down and holds one leg of his briefs open for a foot.

Looking down at him, I know he's right. He did shoot a big wad of cum deep inside me, and it'll just drip down my leg if I don't have something to catch it. I sigh as I slip one stiletto, then the other, into his briefs.

As he pulls them up, I remove his shirt from between my legs. "Just toss it on the floor." He instructs, and when it lands, a big, wet, white spot confirms the size of the load he dumped into me.

As he stands, he pops the waistband. "Good girl."

## Brody

As I bend over and put my pants back on, I smile at her, "You are beautiful, Lizzy."

She cuts her eyes at me as she adjusts her clothes, "You don't have to say that." She looks away, and I sense she thinks I'm just saying it because we fucked.

"Hey. Look at me." I walk over in my bare feet and wait for her to comply. She stops fidgeting with her hair and looks up at me. "I mean it, Lizzy. I think you are beautiful."

She blinks as if stunned by the truth in my eyes and the sincerity in my voice. I leave her staring, walk back to my shoes, and slip my feet into them. Then I pick my shirt up off the floor, roll it up so the wet spot is hidden, and hold my hand out for hers. She walks over and slips it inside. I interlace our fingers, liking how it bonds her to me, and I push the lobby button. The elevator starts down, and we ride in silence.

When the doors slide open, we are greeted by members of the staff. They have obviously been waiting on the elevator and, no doubt, heard me banging Lizzy up against the wall and her screams of ecstasy from the knowing smirks on their faces.

I glance down at her as we walk past them. Her eyes are locked on the floor.

I don't give a shit that everyone who sees us in this state, me half-naked and Lizzy with messy hair, will know we've had wild spontaneous sex, but she's embarrassed and that I care about.

Before we enter the public lobby, I stop, smile down at her, and tell her. "You look radiant right now, but ...." I begin to smooth her stray strands. She stares at me as I work. Her eyes show her appreciation, and a tenderness for her wells up inside.

I tip her face up to mine, "Close your eyes, babe." Then I wipe the smudges of mascara from under her eyes. When I'm finished, I can't resist her pouty lips. I place a peck on them.

She whispers, "Thank you."

*God, this woman! I swear she does it for me!*

# CHAPTER
# FIFTEEN

*Lizzy*

---

We walk silently to my room, arm in arm, and I know the next few minutes will be pivotal in my life. Now that we've fucked, will he say goodbye at the door, or will he want to come inside for more?

We round the corner, and when I see my hotel room, my heart reacts. It starts to race at the thought that this could be goodbye. This could be the last few moments I get to spend with B.A.

I sigh. At least the man of my dreams has a

face now. At least when I dream about finding a man I could love for a lifetime, I can close my eyes and remember him. I take a deep breath to steady my racing heart.

When we arrive, I stare at the door and decide. I will be the one who ends it. Maybe that will make it easier to endure.

My hand reaches into my cleavage for my room key.

"Need some help?" He leans down with a smirk on his face and gets an eyeful.

"No, I got it." I pull the card out and show him. Then I swipe it over the scanner, and the green light on the door handle illuminates. I swallow hard as I push the handle down and step inside. Turning to face B.A., I block his access. "Thanks again for coming to my rescue. I had a great time."

His face freezes, shocked by my words. He wasn't expecting me to give him a way out. I'm sure he's always the one who has to end it. No woman in her right mind would do what I just did. No woman is that crazy.

As I back into my room, my heart reacts to my decision by sending tears to my eyes, and I close them before he can see them. Pushing the door closed, wanting to end it on my terms, I tell him, "Goodbye, B.A."

Dammit! I frown. My voice quivered with emotion.

The door stops.

My eyes open.

B.A.'s outstretched arm, bulging with his beautiful muscles, is blocking the door. I don't want to look into his face, but my heart makes my eyes find his. It wants to know why he is blocking the door. What I see snatches my breath and halts the pounding in my chest.

His face holds nothing but desire for me. Well, desire and confusion. "Lizzy, may I come in?"

"Why?" Falls out of my mouth as my mind fights to protect my heart.

His stunned face steps through the threshold to tower over me. He pinches my chin and forces me to look into his eyes. His intense gaze burns into mine. It feels like he's searching my soul for my secrets. The words on the tip of my tongue, "I'm nothing special," vanish with my breath. "Don't shut me out." He whispers.

And my heart opens up, and tears spill down my face as it shares all the damage done to it by other callous men.

His scowl rips my soul open, then he wraps his arms around me and holds me while I free myself of their scars. Then his lips recapture my mouth, but his kiss is not gentle. His kiss is crushing. Then without asking, he lifts my dress and snatches it off my body. His impatient hands rip my bra off, and my tits bounce free. He drives my body across the room with his as he unzips his pants. When the back of my legs hit the bed, I fall onto it, and he strips naked in a flash.

His incredible body hovers for a moment, then his hands grasp his briefs at my waist, and he pulls them down to my ankles. Gently, he removes my stiletto's, then eases his briefs off. All the while, his eyes have dominated mine.

He places his knee between my legs, and I spread them for him as he climbs on the mattress and hovers over me. The feeling of being owned surges through my being and is followed immediately by the feeling of being home.

He leans down and says, "Grab hold."

I wrap my arms and legs around him, and he

crawls to the center of the bed. He leans back down, and I let go. He places his hands on the inside of my thighs and pushes them open. Then he positions his big, beautiful cock, and tells me, "No talking. Just feeling. Tonight, we make love. Tomorrow, we figure it out."

When he goes down on me, he holds nothing back. He drives himself deep inside with his rhythm, taking what he wants when he wants it. Instead of feeling like a whore being fucked, I feel like a woman being worshipped.

I stop counting my orgasms, losing track of time. When he finally finishes and pulls me to spoon with him, I am happier than I have ever been before. His steady breathing in my ear assures me this was not a dream. This was very real!

---

**Brody**

---

Listening to Lizzy's breath blow softly in her sleep gives me a sense of wholeness. I can't explain how or why it happened, but I'm thankful it did happen. I'm grateful I didn't meet her at John's house. I'm thankful we met as unattached strangers at the dinner show. I'm grateful there was a crisis to rescue her from. And I'm incredibly thankful she opened up and let me see her vulnerability, so I could wipe her slate clean last night.

I kiss her shoulder, and she stirs; then I nibble her ear, and she rolls over onto her back. I whisper, "Good morning."

She smiles at me, and I peck her lips. She slips her arms around my neck and holds my lips against hers. My cock hardens as she opens her mouth, inviting another deep kiss.

When I mount her, she purrs, making me laugh. She's completely submissive, and I take my time between teasing her tits and her clit, until she's moaning for more.

When I slip inside, she groans, "Yes, yes, my God, yes!"

I push away from her embrace and let the length of my cock stroke her. She lifts her face to watch my cock going in and out. I focus on her face, and her expressions tell me precisely what to do. I bring her up, then let her control it before I push her over the edge. When her eyes roll back in her head, I let my orgasm go. Pounding her perfection, I fill her full. Then fall on top of her.

# CHAPTER
# SIXTEEN

*Lizzy*

---

A growling bear wakes me, and I open my eyes. *I'm in a hotel room. How can there be a hungry bear?*

I sit up and look around. B.A. is lying next to me, asleep. His stomach growls, and I giggle. *He's the hungry bear!*

I roll off the bed, grab my phone, and tiptoe to the bathroom. Before I turn the shower on, I place an online order for pizza. Then I submerge under the warm water. I'm just starting to wash my hair when B.A. enters the bathroom. Without asking, he pulls the curtain back and steps inside. I move out from under the water, and he steps under it. We don't talk the entire time we shower, and we don't get aroused. We take our time bathing and getting to know each other's bodies.

As my soapy hands move over his muscles, I can't believe how big and strong he is. Questions begin forming in my mind, and I can't wait to learn about him.

We are drying off when the pizza man knocks. I grin at B.A. "The Pizza-man is here." Then I wrap my towel around myself.

B.A. blocks the door with a look on his face that says, I'm nuts. "YOU are not opening the door!"

I burst out into giggles as he snatches my towel off and wraps it around his waist. Closing the bathroom door behind him, I take his towel and wrap my hair in it. When the room door closes, I open the bathroom door and sniff the air, following the smell of pizza.

He sets it down on the little table, pulls out my chair, then sits down and opens the box. We scarf down the first piece without talking. Then I ask the first question. "What do you do?"

He smirks. "A little bit of everything."

I tilt my head and raise my eyebrows. "If you don't help me out here, this will quickly turn into an interrogation."

He chuckles and takes another bite of pizza. "You first, while I eat."

"Deal." I lean back and pretend I'm at a speed dating table. "My name is Lizzy, short for Liza, but not really. Liza has four letters; Lizzy has five." He laughs as I twitch playfully in my chair. "I'm 26. Single. No kids. I live with my best friend, and I work as a graphic designer at a local sign company."

He nods and continues eating.

"Your turn." I encourage him, but he grins at me. So, I roll my eyes and ask, "What's your name?"

"B.A."

I roll my eyes. "What does B.A. stand for?"

He smirks, "Guess."

I shrug, "I don't know."

He laughs as he takes a huge bite and chews it up, making me wait for his answer. Then he grins that cute boyish grin and says, "B.A. is short for the call name my bros gave me back when. It stands for Badass."

"Oh, damn!" I twinkle at him. "You are definitely that!"

He chuckles. "Yup." Then he motions with his pizza. "I have the perfect call name for you too."

'Really? You don't like Lizzy?"

"Lizzy's ok for everyone else, but I want to have my own special nickname for you."

"What would that be?" I flirt back.

He raises an eyebrow, then gives me a head nod. "I'm going to call you Lizard."

"Lizard?" The Geico lizard pops into my brain. "Lizards are skinny. My curves deserve better than Lizard."

He smirks and looks me up and down. "True that, but your tongue trumps your curves" His eyebrows twitch with his sexy half-smile.

I lick my lips for him, knowing I give excellent head, and he hasn't enjoyed that yet. "Ok," I smirk. "I'll agree to be your Lizard, but I want to give you a special name too."

"I'm digging the name you've already given me." He grabs the legs of my chair and drags me to him as he mimics my orgasmic chant. "Yes, Yes, OH. MY. GOD! Yes!" His voice inflection is spot on, and I blush.

He pulls my body out of the chair and into his lap. He leans back as I straddle him. I poke his chest as his hands slide up my back. "Fair enough. You do fuck like a God, but you also make noises like a Gorilla."

He stops and laughs. "Hell no! I do not!"

"Oh yes, sir, you do." I giggle as I slide off his lap and kneel before him. Then proceed to prove my tongue is like a lizard's, and he does make Gorilla noises when he comes.

---

**Brody**

---

Lying in bed with Lizzy is about as good as it gets. Her soft body is snuggled up against me. I'm amazed at how comfortable we are together. It's like we've always known each other.

She asks, "With a body like yours, you must be or have been in the military."

"Affirmative, but I can't share that with you."

She bites her lip, thinking. "Do you love what you do?"

"I do."

"Can you see yourself doing anything else?"

I think about that for a moment. Until Jeff mentioned his new company, I hadn't, but now, I know I should consider it. If I become an officer, I'm committing long-term to a military career. Which means my family would be committed to it too. I look down at Lizzy; she's so sweet. I can't imagine years of leaving her for six months at a time. But if I join Jeff's group, then I can work as a civilian contractor, have a family, make more money, and still get to do what I love. I smirk. No brainer. I kiss the top of her head. "I can. Jeff offered me a job. I think I'm going to take it."

She squeezes me tight and looks up at me. I smile down at her. "Will you tell me your real name then?"

I flip her over and pull her ass up as I kneel behind her. "Soon, but right now, I'm digging this one," I tell her as I make her chant it for me again.

# CHAPTER SEVENTEEN

*Lizzy*

---

When B.A. walks me out to the car Sunday morning, I feel so incredibly sad. He tosses my backpack in the back, then opens his arms to me.

When I step inside, I can't believe how clingy I am. My arms wrap around his waist, and I hug him tight, trying not to lose my shit. The last thing I want is for him to see me crying over him, but it's damn hard to breathe.

He kisses the top of my head. "Lizard, what's wrong?"

"I'm being stupid again."

He chuckles. "You are not stupid! If I am ever given the opportunity to beat the man's ass that made you believe that about yourself, please let me know. I will relish giving him an ass-whooping for you."

I laugh. "I believe you."

"Now, what's wrong?" He asks again.

"I'm afraid I won't see you again," I confess.

"Babe, I'm sorry. I was wrong. You are being stupid."

I laugh out loud, comforted by his joke. "See, I told you so."

He hugs me tight. "You have my digits. I don't give those out to people I won't see again."

I lean back and look up into his face. "Promise?"

"I have some business to take care of. I'm unsure how long it will take, but you will see me again. I promise."

He pinches my chin and tilts my face up. Then leans down for a farewell kiss. I savor the moment, trying to memorize the look on his face. His eyes, his lips, his scruff because he didn't shave the entire weekend, his smile. The way his tongue feels, the taste of him, the smell of him, the way he makes me feel safe, happy, cherished, appreciated, respected.

When he lets me go, I tell him, "You're my hero, you know."

He chuckles. "Now, that's a special nickname, I'll accept."

I grin at him and know I have completely fallen for his badass.

---

**Brody**

---

I open Lizzy's car door, and she slides in behind the wheel. Then I lean in for a butterfly kiss. She pecks me with duck lips, and I laugh. Ever since I told her how perfect her pouty lips are for pecking, she makes sure I get all she's got.

"Drive careful. Don't speed."

"Yes, sir," she winks at me, then cranks the car. I take a step back and watch my woman drive away. I give her a couple of minutes, then send her a text.

> This is so you believe me. I did give you my digits. I will see you again. Don't text and drive!

I spin around and trot back to the hotel—my phone dings with a text message. Lizzy has sent a screen full of kiss icons.

I rush to my room, change clothes, and throw my gear into my rucksack. Then I run back out and climb into my Corvette. Lizzy will take the interstate back to John's, so I will have to beat her there by taking the scenic route. It is shorter, and I know on Sunday morning, traffic is nonexistent, plus the red lights will be blinking. My GPS calculates I will beat her there by 7 minutes.

As soon as I am outside the city limits, I call Jeff. When he answers, I tell him the news, "I'm in."

"That is fucking fantastic news!" He says. "How soon can you start?"

"I am on 30 days' leave right now. I will call my commander when we hang up and start the paperwork. I should be out before my leave is over."

"Man, timing is everything. I am going to need your expertise immediately."

"What do you need me to do?"

"I need you in Alabama to work up a profile for me."

"That is what I do." I grin, "And I am damn good at it too."

"I'm counting on that." He tells me. "I don't have all the facts yet, but it looks like a snatch and grab by human traffickers. Wheels up in one."

I disconnect the call, then dial my commander. He doesn't answer, so I leave him a message.

While the countryside flies by, I think about being a profiler and what differences I will discover between enemy combatants and civilian bad guys' behaviors. I am good at what I do, and I am excited to prove it to Jeff.

I check the time. I'm two minutes ahead of the original estimated time of arrival.

My mind scans the weekend with Lizzy, and my smile plasters itself on my face. The entire weekend played out better than I could have planned. If she hadn't tried to turn me away, it would have been hard to accomplish so much in so little time. But her insecurities played into my hands. She is everything I have been looking for —the perfect woman for me.

I dial her number.

She answers. "Hey, you!"

"Hey babe, I forgot to tell you to text me when you arrive. I will call you as soon as I can."

"Okay. Perfect." She says, and the word stabs my heart.

"Lizard, is there anything else you want to know about me, other than my real name, that you didn't get to ask?"

"Hmm. Do you have any brothers or sisters?"

I laugh. "I have an older brother, and he is as big a pain in my ass now as he was growing up."

She laughs. "I don't have any siblings, so I can't relate. However, I claim my best friend Tara as my sister from another mister."

"I'm looking forward to meeting her," I tell her. Then I say, "Lizard, I have a question for you."

"What?" She asks.

"Why did you try to turn me away?"

"At the room?"

"Yes."

"Honestly, because you are such a badass. You pushed my panic button."

"Panic button?" I chuckle. "Man, did I miss the mark. I was trying to push your perfect button."

She smiles when she says, "Oh, don't worry, you did push that button. Every time I screamed, 'Yes, Yes, OH. MY. GOD! Yes!'"

# CHAPTER
# EIGHTEEN

### *Lizzy*

---

When I arrive at John's house, I park next to the red corvette. *Great.* I sigh. *John's brother is still here.* Before I open the door, I text B. A.

> I'm here. I'm safe. I miss you bad!

He answers immediately.

> Good. Call you in a few.

> K.

I take a deep breath and prepare to meet Tara's eyes. She knows me better than anyone, and she will know as soon as she lays eyes on me that I have found someone. I open the car door, step out, and text Tara as I walk up to the house.

> I am here.

As soon as I step onto the front porch, the door swings open. Tara stands in the doorway, so excited she is literally twitching.

As I walk up, I try to look natural as I lean in for a hug. She ignores my embrace, grabs my hand, and pulls me inside. Then she shuts the door quietly. She puts her finger over her mouth, telling me to shush.

She steers me to the bathroom down the hall, pushes me inside, then shuts the door just as quietly as she did the front door. When she turns around, she whispers as she inspects my clothes, then examines my face for makeup smears.

"Holy fuck, Lizzy." Her eyes twinkle. "John's little brother is a fucking stud! I mean, like seriously. The man is hotter than John if you can believe that. Like wowzer hot!"

I whisper back to her as she fluffs my curls. "I don't care."

"Well, you should care!" She blows my comment off. "He is tall, built like a brick wall, has beautiful eyes, a handsome face, and a great smile." She shakes her head. "He is the whole damn package!"

I gently take her hands to stop her primping actions and hold them in front of me. I have to let her know I am off the market before we walk out of the bathroom. But I am not sure how to break the news to her. She is not going to want to hear me. She has got her mind made up that this dude and I will be great together.

If I follow her out of here before she knows, she will prance my big ass around, showing me off like an auctioneer. No doubt she has primed the poor dude by singing my praises all weekend.

"Tara. Look at me." I squeeze her fidgety hands. "See how happy I am?" I put my face in front of hers. She stops and looks hard at my expression. Then she narrows her eyes. "I met someone this weekend and have fallen head over heels in love with him!" I smile at her. "And I know it is love because my heart was all over the place."

She presses her lips together and looks at me. "Lizzy, you know I love you, right? And you know you can trust me, right?"

I nod.

"Then, believe me when I tell you, whoever that dude is, he can't hold a candle to who this dude is! I am telling you flat out, girlfriend. He fucking rocked my world, and I am in love with his brother!" She pulls the bathroom door open. "Now, come on. You promised you would meet him before you left on Friday night. He is waiting to meet you."

I shake my head. "I didn't say I wouldn't meet him. I am saying, don't try to hook me up with him. I will be polite, but there is no way anything is going to happen."

She whispers as she drags me out by my arm. "Lizzy, this dude is so fucking hot! You are going to change your mind."

I shake my head harder, following her into the hall. "No. I am not."

When we reach the kitchen, she whispers out of the corner of her mouth, nodding toward the patio. "Lizzy, prepare yourself. He is a fucking stud. I nearly fainted when he walked in." She turns her confident eyes on me.

I grab her by the shoulders and shake her gently. My voice rises above a whisper, demanding her attention. "Tara, you aren't hearing me. I met a man! He is a fucking badass. I spent the entire weekend with his badass. I have fallen in love with his badass."

John yells from the back. "Tara, is that Lizzy?"

I give her a look that says, 'Zip it!'

She grins wickedly at me. "Yes, John, she is here."

"Excellent," he yells. "We are on the patio."

When we round the counter, I see John talking to a man in a baseball cap. He looks up, gives me a head nod, then stands and says to the dude. "There she is." Then he looks back at me and adds, "Come on out here, Lizzy. There is someone I want you to meet."

Reluctantly, I follow Tara onto the patio. The man in the baseball cap stands up as we approach. He and John smile at me, and he holds his hand out. After all, Tara said, I expected more. The dude is handsome, but he is not a fucking stud. I smile politely and shake his hand as John introduces us. "Lizzy, I'd like you to meet Riley Register. Riley, this is Lizzy Mayer, Tara's best friend."

Riley Register? Oh. He isn't John's brother. I shake his hand and say at the same time he does, "It is nice to meet you."

He sits back down, and I look at John. He smiles at me. "Did you have a good weekend?"

"Yes, I did." I grin.

"Better than you expected?"

"Much better than I expected!" I grin at him.

I glance over at Tara, and she explains, "Riley is going to be joining John's pharmaceutical sales team."

"Oh, well, that is great news. Congratulations."

Riley nods, "Thanks. I am excited to start."

Just then, my phone rings. It is B. A. I smile at it and lift it to my ear. "Hey."

"Hey, Lizard, I have a confession to make."

I stand up, holding my hand out to let Tara know this is a private call and I will be right back, but I stop because she is twitching with excitement.

B.A. continues, "I fell in love with you the first time I saw you."

"Hold on, B. A. Let me go to the other room." I turn to go into the kitchen and drop my phone.

My Badass is leaning against the door jam wearing his cute boyish grin. My heart stops beating, and my breath vanishes. He pushes off the wall and walks straight to me.

When he arrives, my heart pounds in my chest, and I still have no breath. He stands tall and proud, towering over me, "But you ran off before I could meet you." He holds his hand out, and like a magnet, mine slips into it. "Allow me to formally introduce myself, Lizard. My name is Brody Andrews. I am John's little brother. My friends call me B.A., but my military bros call me Badass. But you," he pulls me in his arms, leans down, and whispers in my ear, "I prefer you call me, "Yes, Yes. OH. MY. GOD. YES!"

His essence fills every part of me, and I meld into him, then his lips are on mine, and he is pushing all my buttons perfectly.

# EPILOGUE

---

**Brody**

---

I throw my repacked rucksack in the trunk of my car and close the lid. Lizzy is looking at me with a mixture of amazement and fright on her face.

"I'll text you as soon as I know something solid."

She nods.

My phone rings. It's Crockett.

"Yeah," I answer.

"ETA to Live Oak?"

"Touch down is at eighteen hundred hours."

"Roger. There will be someone there to pick you up. I'm forwarding some reading material for your flight."

"Copy that. I'll get up to speed and be ready to roll."

"Good copy. Glad to have you on board, brother. Out here."

I put the phone in my pocket as Lizzy asks, "Where's Live Oak?"

"Alabama." I check my G-shock watch. "I gotta go. I can't miss my flight."

I open my arms, and she rushes into them. Wrapping hers around me and squeezing me tight, she says, "Be safe."

I lift her face to mine and give her a reassuring smile, then gently lay my lips on hers, enjoying her sweet scent and the way she feels so perfect in my arms. "I'll be back as soon as I can, and we'll make plans for our future."

She smiles, then says, "Hurry home. I'll be waiting."

\* \* \*

Thank you for reading Lizzy and Brody's love story.
I hope you enjoyed it and will choose to leave a review for others.
Direct link to Amazon Review:
https://readerlinks.com/l/3626613

The next book is Jeff Crockett's Story.

Target Nina: Ground Zero
https://readerlinks.com/l/3626661

*"This book is one of my **favorite reads.**"* — Goodreads Reviewer

When former Navy SEAL Jeff Crockett sees a suspicious van parked on a residential street in the early morning hours, his instincts kick in. When two men bail out and attempt to snatch a young girl, his training takes over. Without hesitation, he rescues her.

Upon learning she was the random target of sex traffickers, an idea sparks to put together an elite fighting force made up of former Alpha team members to combat this plague facing our citizens.

The first team member to recruit is the key member of Alpha's success. His former targeting officer. Nina 'Foxtrot' Fox. But that's not the only reason she's his first call.

You see, in the military, mission success comes first. Love takes a back seat. But in the civilian world, there are no rules, no restrictions, and no reason for them not to be together.

*"...an action-packed, drama-filled, adrenaline-pumping, chemistry-building storyline."* — *Goodreads Reviewer*

## **Chapter One**

San Diego, California
MARCH 2010
7:00 AM

## Crockett

"Rocket, there's an issue with the beer delivery."

That's the way my morning started at 4:00 o'clock. Instead of heading out for my daily five-mile run, I was in the bar stock room unloading a brand of beer I didn't order but had to accept because my stock was too low to return it.

Three and a half hours later, my schedule is back on track to pound the pavement. It's 7:35 am. I hit the stopwatch on my g-shock watch to track my time as I hit my cruising gait, exiting the parking lot of *Suds After BUD/S* Bar.

The highway traffic isn't congested yet. However, it is heavy enough and will only intensify as rush-hour approaches. It'll be safer running through the residential area this time of day. Parents are more aware of pedestrians with school buses and carpools.

Good choice, I phrase myself as I cruise between the streets and the sidewalks, leaving the first subdivision behind and entering the second one.

As soon as I run through the entrance, I spot a white work van, and my SEAL sixth sense alarm bells go off. It's out of place. Granted, it may be a work crew arriving early to repair someone's plumbing or an electrical issue, but my gut tells me it isn't.

I jog onto the sidewalk and stop behind a tree to observe without being seen.

There are no identifying markings on the side of the van. Two men have their forearms resting in the open windows. Nothing unusual or alarming. Except they are wearing black hoodies, and it's not cool this morning.

Not convinced I'm wrong yet, I hang back to observe them.

In the next few minutes, the neighborhood comes alive with organized chaos as adults and children exit their homes. Some load into their vehicles and drive away. While others hang out in their front yards, waiting for their ride to pick them up, chatting with their next-door neighbors, or looking at their phones. All are unaware that danger may be lurking in the white van. No one pays it any attention.

When the school bus turns onto the street at the opposite end of the block, children move to the curb along the street, waiting for their turn to board the bus.

As soon as the van's engine comes to life and the brake lights glow an ominous warning, years of extensive training as a SEAL kick in, and the hair on the back of my neck rises as I identify the intentions of the men in the van. This is a brazen snatch-and-grab in broad daylight.

I scan the neighborhood for their target. Two houses away, I spot her. A young pre-teen girl slings a heavy backpack onto her shoulders and moves to her designated pickup point.

There is time to let my presence be known and scare the would-be kidnappers away before they make their move, and as a civilian, I should make that choice. But I also know that doing so will, more than likely, *not* be a deterrent from a future attempt. It's quite possible they will just move to a different neighborhood when I've moved on.

Or do I sit tight and let them hang the crime around their necks? Then stop them before they can get away? It's tough because this choice leads to the young girl being traumatized but safe.

I pull my weapon from my shoulder holster

and wait behind the tree, watching how they will carry out their mission.

I have no official authority to act in any capacity. But I can't turn off who I am. I'm a special warfare operator trained to defend Americans' right to live free and to protect those who cannot protect themselves. I will continue to serve as a guardian of freedom.

The bright red brake lights vanish as the van begins to creep forward. The young girl is looking at her phone, oblivious to her surroundings, as she stops at the edge of the curb.

That's when all hell breaks loose. The side sliding door and the passenger cab door swing open, and two men bail out, charging the unsuspecting girl.

The calm of battle settles over me as my training controls my response to their chaos. Every sense is heightened. Every movement is composed—every decision is backed by discipline.

When the men are a few feet away from her, she looks up from her phone. Shocked, she freezes. Before she can flee, they are on her.

The first man dry-tases her, and she jerks from the jolt of electricity, dropping her phone.

Momentarily stunned, the shift of her backpack's weight causes her young, underdeveloped body rigged from the voltage to keel over.

My subconscious begins a count of her trauma to exact vengeance for her. They will pay for that.

The men each grab an arm and drag her toward the van. She regains her wits and starts kicking and screaming, putting up one hell of a fight for a little thing, and the commotion she's causing is the perfect cover for me to rush up to the back of the van unseen.

The entire crew is focused on getting the flailing girl fighting for her life inside the vehicle as fast as possible so they can disappear with her when I step around the side of the van. In two strides, I'm next to her, with my weapon pointed less than three feet from the face of the man inside who is hoisting her in by her hair.

"Hooyah, Motherfuckers, not on my watch."

The driver of the van yells, "WHAT THE FUCK?"

As the three men attacking her freeze with surprise, then fear. Their grips loosen. The frightened, fighting girl breaks free, fleeing to the safety of her home, screaming for her mama.

The driver of the van yells again, "SHIT!"

Staring at my pistol pointed at his frozen accomplices, his eyes flare in fear, then flash panic right before he makes a deadly decision, reaching for his pistol lying on the center console. As his hand encircles it, I hit him with a single shot between his eyes. His head snaps back as the bullet enters, then recoils forward from the force of his skull exploding. His brain splatters on the steering wheel and windshield.

―――――

*Nina*

―――――

Standing at the front door, watching Jeff Crockett hold three men at gunpoint outside a white van parked at the curb while Bethany, my twelve-year-old niece, races across the yard to us, calling her mama like a three-year-old, is the biggest mind fuck of my life.

We were sitting at the kitchen table, enjoying a cup of coffee, discussing our plans for the day, when we heard a gunshot. The sound sent a wave of sheer terror through us, and we jumped to our feet, then charged the front door. Our lives forever changed.

In shock on multiple levels, I'm rooted to the spot. Maternal emotion for the girl I love, as if she were my own, dumps adrenaline in my blood while fierce passion for the man I love who is in danger courses through my veins. Ultimately, my training kicks in to assess the situation.

Bethany is safe in Bri's arms. Crockett has the perps apprehended. I step back inside and usher my sister and niece in, closing the door on the team leader of Alpha. The man that I served alongside as their targeting officer. The man I fell in love with, but the man who never knew due to military restrictions against relationships between team members.

Now is not the time for a reunion with Crockett. Now my family comes first.

———

Crockett

———

Immediately, my weapon returns to my first target's face, and sheer terror stares back at me. A dark wet spot grows at his groin. He's pissed himself.

Before any of the remaining three choose to make a deadly decision, I command them, "Put your hands on your head. Interlace your fingers."

In shock and fear, they do what they are told.

"Step out of the van. Drop to your knees."

They obey, but I know the adrenaline rush will hit them at any moment, and nature will make them choose fight or flight, and I prepare to pull the trigger again.

Taking a commanding, menacing step toward them to counteract their adrenaline dump, I give them their only option. "Kiss the ground that little girl walked on, and don't fucking move a goddamn muscle, or I will blow your fucking brains out like your compadre's there. Do you understand?"

The forcefulness of my vow makes them fall on their faces, and we wait for the police to arrive without further incident.

## Nina

While Bri comforts her daughter, I watch from the window as the men lie face down with Rocket standing guide over them, waiting for the police to arrive. He's a beautiful sight to behold. Standing there in all his SEAL glory with the situation under control.

My heart flutters watching him, confirming my fear that even after years apart, he's the one that rocks my world. I look at my niece, safe in my sister's arms, and dread the inevitable outcome. I must thank Rocket for rescuing my niece. But I honestly don't know if my broken heart can take the face-off with him if it leads to nothing more than friendship. I am and always will be in love with him.

## Crockett

In no time, two police cruisers are on site.

As soon as the police officers exit their vehicles, I drop to my knees, place my weapon on the ground, and put my hands on my head, interlocking my fingers.

After the police take control of the chaos, I give my statement, and witnesses come forward, reiterating what I have testified.

Before I leave, I look at the little girl's house. She and her mother stand in the doorway, watching, and someone else is standing in the shadow at the window. The young girl raises her hand to wave a silent thank you, and I raise mine in response.

Freedom is always worth fighting for.

Continue reading:
Target Nina
https://readerlinks.com/l/3626661

# COQ BLOCKERS SECURITY TEAM

**Jeff Crockett, aka Rocket**
*Target Nina*
Chief Executive Officer (CEO)
Mission Team Leader
Former Navy SEAL Tier One
Special Warfare Operator
Alpha 1
Height: 6'5"
Weight: 260

**Maximus Aurelius Moore, aka Hardcore**
*Mr. Sexy in 9G*
Chief Financial Officer (CFO)

Billionaire Investor
Former Army Aviator
Apache and Blackhawk Pilot
Height: 6'0"
Weight: 200 lbs

### Nina Fox, aka Foxtrot
*Target Nina*
Chief Operating Officer (COO)
Mission Team Commander
Former Tier One Targeting Officer
For Alpha Team

### Meghan Meadows, aka Ambassador
Chief Liaison Officer (CLO)
Mission Coordination Team Member
Former Army ISA Officer

### Mike Franks, aka Mr. Mom
Mission Team Member
Former Navy SEAL Tier One
Special Warfare Operator
Alpha 2
Height: 6'0"
Weight: 200 lbs

### Jack Black, aka Hammer

*Target Logan*
Mission Team Member
Former Navy SEAL Tier One
Special Warfare Operator
Alpha 3
Height: 6'1"
Weight: 230

### Jocko Malone, aka Fastball

*Coming Home For Her*
Mission Team Member
Special Warfare Operator
Former Navy SEAL Tier One
Special Warfare Operator
Alpha K9 handler
Height: 6'4"
Weight: 250

### Lucifer, aka Luce

*Coming Home For Her*
Mission Team Member
Special Warfare Operator
Former Navy SEAL
Belgian Malinois

Multipurpose K9

### **Brody Andrews, aka Badass**
*Target Lizzy*
Mission Team Member
Special Warfare Operator
Former Navy SEAL Tier Two
Special Warfare Operator
Height: 6'3"
Weight: 265 lbs

### **Justin Davis, aka Danger**
*Moving Back For Her*
Mission Team Member
Former Marine
Height: 6'3"
Weight: 230

### **Zane Lockhart, aka Insane**
*Making Good For Her*
Mission Team Member
Special Warfare Operator
Former Navy SEAL Tier Two
Special Warfare Operator
Deputy Sheriff - K9 handler

Height: 6'1"
Weight: 210

### Batman, aka Bruce Wayne
*Making Good For Her*
Mission Team Member
Law Enforcement
Belgian Malinois
Multipurpose K9

### Dirk Sam, aka Sam-I-Am
*Manning Up For Her*
Mission Air Support Team Member
Former Army Aviator
Apache and Blackhawk Pilot
Height: 6'2"
Weight: 225

### Micah Young, aka Dark Thirty
Mission Technical Support Team Member
CIA Agent - Hacker

### License To Own
Mission Team Overwatch
Drone Operator

Civilian Video Gamer

**Nikolai Smirnov, aka Grappler**
*Opening Up For Her*
Mission Team Hand-to-Hand Combat Trainer
Former MMA Champion Fighter
Height: 5'10"
Weight: 185

## JESSIKA WRITING AS STINGRAY23
HOT MILITARY ROMANTIC SUSPENSE

### **A Few Good Men**

Target Lizzy

Target Nina

Target Logan

Target Marie

Target Bella

# JESSIKA WRITING AS CINDEE BARTHOLOMEW

### **The Liotine Heir**

American Flyboy

Italy's Most Eligible Bachelor

### **Worth The Risk Series**

Secret Life

Stunning Secret

Shocking Secret

Dark Secret

Twisted Secret

Startling Secret

### **Standalone**

Twisted To Get Her

# READ JESSIKA'S NEWEST, SEXIEST, AND MOST TALKED ABOUT BESTSELLERS...

## LIFE IN LIVE OAK

*Coming Home For Her*

*Moving Back For Her*

*Manning Up For Her*

*Opening Up For Her*

*Making Good For Her*

## SUCH A BOSS

*Big Book Boss*

*Big Booze Boss*

## BILLION HEIR

*Fraudulent Fiancee*

*Escaping in Glass Slippers*

*Accidental Amnesia*

## THE HARDCORE NOVELS:

## SPECIAL EDITIONS

*Untouchable Billionaire*

*Unstoppable Billionaire*

*Unforgettable Billionaire*

## THE HARDCORE COLLECTION:

## TRILOGY BOXSETS

*Undeniable Chemistry*

*Unbridled Passion*

*Unwavering Devotion*

## THE HARDCORE SERIES:

## ORIGINAL SIRI'S SAGA

*Mr. Sexy in 9G*

*The Cock-Tail Party*

*The Perfect Man*

*It's Ladies Night*

*The Battle is On*

*The Sex Pot*

*In Heaven at Last*

*A Shakeup Occurs*

*He's Hard Core*

*The End of Her*

*A Shakedown Happens*

*Family First Always*

Learn more at

JessikaKlide.com

# STINGRAY23

Top 4 Amazon Chart author of HOT romcoms Jessika Klide's alter ego, Stingray23 pens HOT Military Romantic Suspense Thrillers.

---

#4 Amazon Chart Author of HOT billionaire romance brings her readers the perfect blend of heat, humor, and heart.

## JOIN JESSIKA'S VIP READER'S LIST

for exclusive giveaways, new release information, sales, and more.
https://jessikaklide.com/

Newsletters not your thing?
No worries.
**— CONNECT ON SOCIAL MEDIA —**

- goodreads.com
- facebook.com/JessikaKlideRomance
- instagram.com/jessikaklideauthor
- bookbub.com/authors/jessika-klide
- x.com/JessikaKlide
- tiktok.com/@authorjessikaklide

Stingray23.com

JessikaKlide.com

Made in the USA
Monee, IL
24 January 2024